THE UNEXPECTED STORM

THE FRIESSEN LEGACY

THE OUTSIDER SERIES

LORHAINNE ECKHART

The Unexpected Storm Copyright © 2013 Lorhainne Ekelund
The Unexpected Storm Paperback Copyright © 2022 Lorhainne Ekelund
Editor: Talia Leduc

ISBN - 13: 978-1990590931
Give feedback on the book at:
lorhainneeckhart.le@gmail.com

Twitter: @LEckhart
Facebook: AuthorLorhainneEckhart

Printed in the U.S.A

THE FRIESSEN FAMILY SERIES READING ORDER:

The Outsider Series

The Forgotten Child (Brad and Emily)
A Baby And A Wedding
Fallen Hero (Andy, Jed, and Diana)
The Search
The Awakening (Andy and Laura)
Secrets (Jed and Diana)
Runaway (Andy and Laura)
Overdue
The Unexpected Storm (Neil and Candy)

The Wedding (Neil and Candy)

The Friessens: A New Beginning

The Deadline (Andy and Laura)
The Price to Love (Neil and Candy)
A Different Kind of Love (Brad and Emily)
A Vow of Love, A Friessen Family Christmas

The Friessens

The Reunion
The Bloodline (Andy & Laura)
The Promise (Diana & Jed)
The Business Plan (Neil & Candy)
The Decision (Brad & Emily)
First Love (Katy)
Family First
Leave the Light On
In the Moment
In the Family: A Friessen Family Christmas
In the Silence
In the Stars
In the Charm
Unexpected Consequences
It Was Always You
The First Time I Saw You
Welcome to My Arms
Welcome to Boston (A Paige & Morgan Short Story)
I'll Always Love You
Ground Rules
A Reason to Breathe
You Are My Everything
Anything For You

The Homecoming
When They Were Young (Link included FREE with The
Homecoming)
Stay Away From My Daughter
The Bad Boy
A Place of Our Own
The Visitor
All About Devon
Long Past Dawn
How to Heal a Heart
Keep Me In Your Heart

The Friessen Family

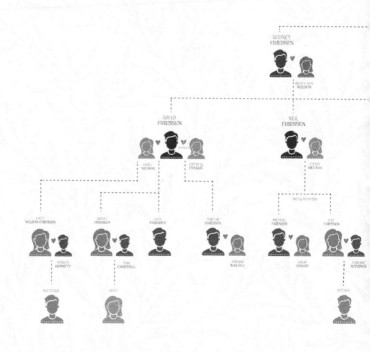

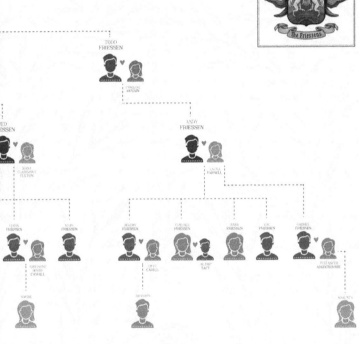

...riessens

THE ENTIRE FRIESSEN FAMILY
ANDY & LAURA
JED & DIANA
NEIL & CANDY
BRAD & EMILY
KATY & STEVEN
KATY & STEVEN

The Friessens

LEAVE THE LIGHT ON
IN THE MOMENT
IN THE FAMILY
IN THE SILENCE
IN THE STARS
IN THE CHARM
UNEXPECTED CONSEQUENCES

KATY & STEVEN
BECKY & TOM
THE ENTIRE FRIESSEN FAMILY
CAT & XANDER
DANNY & EVIE
CHRIS & ED
CHRIS & ED

The Friessens

IT WAS ALWAYS YOU
THE FIRST TIME I SAW YOU
WELCOME TO MY ARMS
WELCOME TO BOSTON
I'LL ALWAYS LOVE YOU
GROUND RULES
A REASON TO BREATHE
YOU ARE MY EVERYTHING
ANYTHING FOR YOU
THE HOMECOMING

KATY & STEVEN
GABRIEL & ELIZABETH
CHELSEA & ALARIC
PAIGE & MORGAN
JEREMY
JEREMY & TIFFY
TREVOR & JASMINE
MICHAEL & ANGIE
THE ENTIRE FRIESSEN FAMILY

—"The brothers are all headstrong and hot but each has a vulnerability that makes the strong women they seek to take a second look. Save this one for last and read the others first. You won't be disappointed."

— KAREN

—"Wish there were truly men in the world like the Friessen men."

— SARA

—"I love the Friessen men. I really love each story and I hope they keep coming."

— MICHELE

—"I can't wait for the last book of this series. The Friessen clan is an interesting one and I have thoroughly enjoyed them all. I love that Neil finally found someone to love. A great story."

— PETRA, A. REVIEWER

He can have any woman, except the one he wants.

She's heartbroken and alone. He can have any woman except the one he wants. Trapped together by a storm could be their only salvation.

In *THE UNEXPECTED STORM*, Candy McRae is barely making ends meet. She's heartbroken and alone and when Neil Friessen offers to buy her property she refuses. Even though he could solve all her problems, she'd rather sell to the devil himself.

Smart and sexy Neil Friessen is quite the catch. He's wealthy, stubborn, arrogant and thoughtful. He attracts women, and million dollar deals, and plans to build a resort on the property next to his. The only thing standing between him and his sweet deal is the dark haired beauty who owns the property he wants.

When a storm forces everyone to evacuate Candy refuses to leave. But it's Neil who shows up, Neil who rescues her. Except by the time he finds her, they can't get out. Neil is alone with the one woman he's always wanted. And he'll have to choose between this dark haired beauty that fills his dreams every night, and building his million dollar resort.

CHAPTER
ONE

E very once in a while, your heart has a mind of its own. It aches, it weeps, but there are days it soars and pumps with so much joy that you want to shout out to everyone just how wonderful everything is: The sun is perfect, the stars have all lined up, and you feel absolutely mind-blowingly freaking fantastic. The heart can also be responsible for you doing the most stupid, dumb-ass things ever, such as sliding your arms around the first good-looking babe you see and leaning in to taste her sweet lips with an out-of-this-world kiss that zings rockets right through your body, blowing off the top of your head, further proving you've checked your brain in to the nearest broom closet.

Maybe that was why Neil Friessen was standing barefoot, his shirt wide open, with the stinging outline of the sexiest hand imprinted on his face, after being slapped by the dark-haired babe he'd just kissed. She was drop-dead gorgeous, even with those smoky brown eyes sizzling with the fires of hell and shooting sparks his way. She had the most stunning set of long dark lashes, full rosy lips, a narrow nose, cheekbones that shaped her oval face, and a strong jaw. My God, this woman had him, Neil Friessen, a tall, "smart and sexy"—the exact words his sister-in-law Diana had used to describe him—man taking a nosedive in the dirt like some fumbling twenty-year-old. And Neil was definitely not fumbling or twenty.

Neil always had women hitting on him anywhere he went, and he loved it. It stoked his ego and made him feel damn good, not to mention he loved the ladies, especially those with mile-long legs and thick dark hair that had that bedroom look, as if he'd just run his fingers through those luscious locks. That was the babe standing before him on the sandy banks of the Gulf of Mexico, about thirty miles northwest of Cancun on the Yucatan Peninsula, where the forest met the ocean and where her horse, a beautiful smoky gray Azteca gelding, was ground tied on the sandy beach.

It wasn't as if he didn't know who she was: Candy McCrae, the daughter of Randy McCrae. Her father had bought this spectacular piece of paradise, two hundred acres of beach and rainforest, a property Neil had been trying to get his hands on for five years. The property backed onto the ten-thousand-acre parcel that Neil owned with his father, Rodney, and it was the missing key to their own paradise, the exact spot where Neil planned to build his five-star resort.

"Just what was that?" she spit out, and he could see the way she struggled to breathe, as if she'd just gone three rounds in a fight.

"Sorry. Lost my head is all, Candy. My brother Jed and his wife had a baby. Just got the news." Neil held up his cell phone as if to show her he was telling the truth.

She didn't cry or yell. What she did was fist her hands as if she was going to come at him again and pop him in the mouth this time, not that he didn't deserve it. But, hell, he'd wanted to kiss Candy as far back as he could remember. The trouble was that she hated him. No, it wasn't hate —it was the fact that she wished he'd die some horrible, painful death. He was pretty sure those had been her exact words when he asked her out for dinner two years ago and then a second time when he saw her in Cancun, getting supplies, eight months ago. That time, she had added in the "Drop dead" look she'd mastered just for him, and she did so every time since he tried to talk to her.

"Let me get this straight. Because you get news of something great happening in your life, your family, it gives you the right to trespass on my property, sneak up behind me, grab me, and kiss me. Or is there something else you're planning to do to ruin my life?" she snapped.

Her words were the second slap Neil had received in the past five minutes, and then it hit him: the vile, disgusting realization that she thought he, Neil Friessen, who could have any woman he wanted, was trying to force himself on her.

Hell, no! It was the first time he actually stuttered and backed up, waving his hands in front of him. "No, no, I don't think so. You got this all wrong, Candy." Then he rammed his fingers through his thick brown hair and took another step back. "Look, Candy, I am sorry. I just saw you sitting there...." Had he lost his mind? He almost said he'd wanted to taste her lips and take them for a test drive for as far back as he could remember. She'd looked so lost and innocent, sitting there in the sand, when he stepped over the dune and saw her. "Well, you stood up, and when you turned to face me, you had a look on your face as if you wanted me to kiss you. I kind of lost my head."

Neil didn't think she could get any angrier, but he was wrong. Her mouth gaped, and she appeared to lean closer, as if she was getting ready to blast him. Then she shut her mouth and crossed her arms tightly to her chest, tapping her foot.

"I was excited, and, my God, you were just there...."

"So you thought you could, what, have some fun with me? A romp in the sand and then send me on my way?" She gave him her back and stormed toward her horse, a few yards away.

"No, Candy, wait. I was actually on my way over to talk to you when I got this call. Look, I'm sorry." This was not going well. Neil was a master at working people, wooing women, and getting what he wanted. He'd always had a silver tongue, and he knew just the right thing to say and the perfect time to say it. He could always make everyone feel good about themselves, even when life dumped shit all around him. He saw the good in everything, including this feisty broad who stared at him as if he were a disease she had no intention of catching. Neil's sharp-witted tongue and nimble mind, which he counted on to talk him out of this mess with Candy, were, for the first time in his life, blank.

"Look, I want to talk to you about your property. I heard you went to Francisco Kan and asked him for help, offered him part ownership of your land, your property here." Neil swept his hand out in a dramatic gesture, but she stopped and spun around, planting both fists on her slim, sexy hips, which were exactly where his eyes went. She wore light khaki pants with a drawstring tie and a short sleeveless tee that showed her belly button and pale, flat abs.

"What? How the hell would you know anything about that?" She smacked her hand to her forehead as if she had realized something. "Why, that son of a bitch! Just what the hell did Francisco do, go running to you after he turned me down?"

"Is that what he did, turn you down?" Neil couldn't believe she wouldn't have come to him. When she didn't answer, instead staring at him in a way that let him know she had shut down, he was certain something more was going on. He knew she struggled, and he didn't know how she made ends meet. When Francisco, a short, dark-haired Mayan in his late fifties, had come to him that morning and mentioned in his very calm way, without disclosing whatever it was that Candy was trying to hide, that she had come to him to ask him to invest in her property, well, Neil had decided to go and see Candy.

He should have known better, except he couldn't help worrying about her. He cared, even though she'd kicked him in the nuts one time after another, and he couldn't figure out what he'd done that had her loathing him. It bothered him, and he'd lost sleep over it, because she was the one woman who could push every single one of his buttons, turning bubbly and sharp-witted Neil Friessen into a raving lunatic.

"Look, I just want to talk to you. Would you come back here?"

"What do you want?" She made no move toward him. In fact, he could see every muscle in her arm tighten, and if he dared to step any closer to her, she'd probably deck him again.

"Candy, I've made you several generous offers to buy your property, and you've turned me down each time. If you're looking for a partner, I'd love to sit down with you and discuss it...."

"Oh, I just bet you would." She cut him off, grinding her teeth and spitting out each word. "Well, let me tell you something, Neil Friessen: I don't want you as a partner. I would rather go into business with the devil himself than have anything to do with the likes of you. Now get the hell off my property." She jabbed her finger angrily to the tree line and the path he'd taken to walk there.

"What the hell did I ever do to you, Candy? I can't for the love of God figure you out, woman," Neil snapped. As he scrambled to think, he was sure he'd never done anything inappropriate. He liked her, he wanted to date her, and she fascinated him.

Candy narrowed those smoldering eyes, and this time he knew he'd get blasted. "You are a piece of work, Neil Friessen. You destroy people, you buy people, and you walk all over them if you don't get what you want. You use them and toss them away as if they're nothing, but you won't ever get that chance with me."

Candy stomped toward her horse, picking up the lead rope and looping it around his neck. His long mane appeared freshly brushed, and Neil wondered why she never trimmed it. They were both wild in a beautiful, mesmerizing way, completely in sync with each other, reading and anticipating one another's movements. He could actually picture the feeling of love between them. She mounted easily, riding bareback, and then turned her horse, staring down at Neil with the same blazing anger. It was so intense that even her horse sidestepped and pranced.

"If I find you on my property again, I'll shoot you." She kicked her horse and took off in a canter down the sandy beach to where her small two-bedroom home had been built just inside the shelter of the trees.

Neil watched, completely dumbstruck by her. His unbuttoned cotton shirt rustled in the breeze, and he rubbed his hand over light brown chest hair, wondering what the hell she thought he'd done. He spit on the ground. "Well, good riddance."

He was so done. He had come over here to offer his help, and she had practically spit on him again. Well, no more. He was so over her. He wasn't a masochist, so why did he keep acting as if he were? It was time he moved on and stopped thinking about her and allowing his guts to get so knotted up over her. He'd date other women, sure one of the two dozen women who'd been flirting with him for months would distract him. At least they appreciated who he was and what he had to offer. He was a fine catch, and he just knew one of them would interest him. Tonight would be the first night of the rest of his life.

CANDY SPURRED HER HORSE ON. "Come on, Sable!" she shouted. She leaned forward, racing over the thick white sand. The salty air mixed with the sound of the waves crashing against the shore, and she wanted to run and run. Her horse was responding, flying along with her. "Whoa, easy, boy." She sat heavier to slow the horse until he walked, and he snorted, breathing heavily just like she was.

They were completely in sync, understanding each other, her and her beautiful gray horse. He had reacted to her jolt of anger at Neil Friessen, her fury, her rage, and she knew better than to allow her blood to boil and her every emotion to spin out of control around her horse.

Being around Neil was an emotional roller coaster. She wanted to hate him, but every time she saw him, his presence shot fire right through her. She tried to tell herself it was because he was the best-looking man in these parts. Attraction and sexuality oozed out of him in a boy-next-door, best-friend kind of way. He had silky short brown hair and a strong, powerful face that reminded her of all those hot movie stars, but his eyes were the color of whiskey, endless, always dancing with a spark of light. Every time she saw him, she couldn't shake the image of him looking down on her in bed, and then she'd be furious at herself for going down that road—even though he had a body she'd love to explore, with tight abs and pecs under shirts that fit tastefully against his biceps. Lord, with those broad shoulders, it was clear the man worked out, but he probably owned some fancy home gym with a personal trainer and all.

She pulled up to the corral where she kept her horses and slid off Sables' back, hitting the ground. He was sixteen hands high, a big boy, all solid muscle, but he was sweet and loyal, and he always knew what she was thinking. He nuzzled her cheek, and she kissed his muzzle and patted his shoulder before loosely tying him to the corral fence.

As she brushed her horse down softly, she had to remind herself that Neil Friessen was just playing with her, and it hurt like hell. She wanted to be loved, not toyed with, and she knew the only reason he was nice to her and was pursuing her, all flirty and interested, was because he wanted her land. The first time he asked her out, her dad had still been alive, and he warned her that they were sitting on prime real estate and that the Friessens wanted their property. Going out with Neil would only get her heart broken, because he had an agenda. Her dad had said that Neil would do anything to get their property, even pretend an interest in Candy. She'd listened thankfully, even though it stung beyond belief, because she wanted his interest to be genuine. The last time she saw Neil, he'd just finished with some blonde, carrying her bag and setting it in a cab, hugging her. Then he'd spotted Candy. Candy had been stunned, because she couldn't believe he had the gall to ask her on a date less than five minutes after he'd been with another woman. Although she was proud of what she'd said, telling him to drop dead, she really wanted to hate him. It would be easier, and her heart would stop flip-flopping from her toes to her head every time she saw him. Even today she'd been embarrassed by how much she wanted that kiss, which was why she'd slapped him as hard as she could. She had known he was there, striding behind her, and when she stood up, her heart had flipped a switch, as if lightning zinged through her when his lips touched hers.

She touched her swollen lips, still burning, and licked the taste of Neil from them. It was so much like the sweetest dessert she anticipated and loved, and she wanted seconds. But she couldn't have firsts, and she couldn't have seconds, so she watched her horse prancing in the corral with her two other horses, a dark thoroughbred and a palomino, and she focused on her problems, wondering what she'd have to sell next to buy their feed, to pay the farrier and the local vet. There, it had worked, and she felt like absolute crap.

CHAPTER
TWO

"Look, Candy, I know you love this place, it's part of you, yadda yadda, but..." Vibrant, redheaded Stella Delinsky, Candy's banker, looked completely out of place standing in the dusty dirt yard in front of the small adobe home. She wore bright red heels, a green pencil skirt, and a paisley blouse, with a red scarf draped around her short, vibrant curls. She was a seventy-year-old woman who didn't give a crap where she was and handled anything and everything with an "It is what it is" attitude.

Candy carried a bucket of water to the squared-out corral where her horses were kicking up dust and swishing their tails to knock the flies off as a two-week-old baby donkey dogged her heels.

"What the hell is that?" Stella barked as she set her hands on her plump hips.

"This is Ambrose. Isn't he cute?" Candy set down the bucket and petted the baby donkey as it rubbed against her leg. She bent down and kissed the top of its head, and it jumped around excitedly and stumbled on the long, gangly donkey legs that it had yet to grow into. "I found him on my way back from town two weeks ago. His mother was hit by a tour bus, and the damn thing just drove away, left her to die. There was Ambrose, at the side of the road. He still had the afterbirth on him. I think he was only a few hours old. I couldn't save his mama, but I brought this guy home with me, fed him goats' milk from a bottle, and look at him now!"

Stella slid her dark glasses down her large nose and peered at Candy with soft blue eyes, staring at her as if she thought she'd lost her mind. "Of course you did. For the love of God, you can barely feed yourself, you've not a dime to your name, and you're picking up strays and bringing them home. What the heck are you doing here, girl?"

Candy knew no one would understand, so she simply sighed, picked up the bucket of water, and kept going, filling the tub for the horses.

"Look at you. You're working yourself to the bone. You have nothing coming in, Candy. Every resource you had is gone, and you're down to how many horses? There are no more tourists booking trail rides with you. They've gone to the bigger guy. What's his name, anyway?" Stella snapped her fingers as she did when trying to remember something. "That guy on the other side of Cancun?"

"Nate Bradley." Candy knew exactly who he was, a dark-haired Texan, someone else she hated.

"Ah, yes, Nate, great businessman. He's landed a contract with all the cruise ships that come in. Touristy stuff. Candy, I hate to tell you this, honey, but maybe you need to sell off part of this land. Come on, honey. Your dad's been gone for over a year now. You're going to kill yourself working, and how safe is it out here for a single woman?" Stella flicked her hand in the air, her long artificial nails painted bright red, a statement of her and who she was.

"I'm fine out here, Stella. I grew up here and can manage just fine." She wiped her forehead, and her white sleeveless tank was stained with grime and sweat.

"Honey child, you're not fine. That's why I'm here. You're in arrears on the mortgage, and..."

"I'll get you the money. I just need some time. I have a couple buyers lined up for the horses, and then I'll have enough to get me caught up and then some." Candy swallowed the lump in her throat as she watched the horses she loved so much. They hadn't provided any income for trail rides on the beach for a long time, not since that other guy moved in. The greedy bastard had bought a stable of horses and taken all the business. Maybe he was in cahoots with Neil, running her out of business so Neil could pick up her land for a dime.

"You're selling Sable? I thought you'd never part with him."

"No, I'd never sell Sable. My dad bought him for me. It's the other two." Candy watched Melody, the palomino, and Frank, the thoroughbred. She had worked with them for the past few years, a five- and six-year-old, and they were in good health, well trained. She just hoped the wealthy American who wanted them came through.

She heard the heavy sigh behind her. "Candy, I love you, darling, I really do. Call Neil Friessen, and we'll work something out with him. He's always wanted to buy this place, and I'm sure you could sell part and have enough to look after your strays and stay here, although I can't figure out why you would. You're young, gorgeous. Move into town, get yourself a condo, meet some guys, have some fun. You know Neil is interested in you."

"No!" She pumped her fists and tossed the bucket,

scaring her baby donkey, who raced away and almost hid behind Stella. "Not him. He's the scum of the earth, after what he did to my dad. He was responsible for my dad's death. If it wasn't for him..."

"Candy, Neil didn't have anything to do with your dad dying." Stella cut her off. "I hate to tell you this, honey, but your dad drank himself to death. No one had him swallow all those pills with that booze except he himself."

Candy turned away because she didn't want to listen to this. Her dad may have swallowed all those pills, but it was Neil who had forced him to that point. Her dad had even said Neil wanted their property so badly he'd do anything to get it, that it was Neil who was responsible for their troubles. She believed her father when he said that Neil had forced them into the financial mess they were in. Her dad had so many debts, and after his charter business for offshore fishing and scuba-diving tours all dried up, she knew it had all been because of Neil. Her dad said Neil had threatened him, saying he'd find a way to get a hold of this property and that he kept low-balling him with a ridiculous offer.

"Candy, listen to me. I liked Randy. He was a character, but he was also the biggest bull-shitter around. He could spin a tale about anyone he didn't like, and he had his hands in things that I wonder if you even know about. You need to start seeing the situation for what it really was. Open your eyes, girl, because I think you've misjudged Neil. He has a good heart, and I know he cares about you. I know he's concerned about you, out here."

"Stella, the man has a heart of stone, and the only concern he has for me is how he can steal my land away and put up his fancy resort, probably right where my house is!" Candy yanked open the wooden shed and lifted the lid off the sealed bin that held the grain for the horses. She scooped some into a pail and strode back across the dusty dirt yard to the corral, not missing the frown on Stella's face. "Just give me until the end of the week, Stella. I'll have the money."

"Candy, I love you, honey, and if it were up to me, I would give you all the time you need, but I can't keep carrying you. I'll give you two days, and then I want you to talk to Neil." Stella strode in those four-inch heels on the uneven ground as if she were in a ballroom. Those shoes were downright sexy, but Candy knew that if they were on her size-eight feet, she'd probably break her ankle. Stella strode around on those spikes as if she'd been born in them.

"I mean it, Candy. Two days and you call me. I'll go with you to see Neil, but you've run out of options, honey." Stella strode up to Candy and held both her shoulders, then air-kissed both her cheeks. "Okay, I gotta go. I'll leave you to your strays, but a word of advice: If you see any more, keep driving."

Candy said not a word as she stood in the middle of the yard, watching the dust cloud from Stella's Land Rover trail behind her as she drove away. Candy knew hell would freeze over before she'd ever allow Neil Friessen to own one inch of her property.

CHAPTER
THREE

"Stella, this is a surprise! What brings you to my part of paradise?" Neil asked as he dried himself off with a fluffy blue towel after climbing out of the Olympic-sized saltwater pool at the back of his sprawling adobe mansion.

"Neil, if I were thirty years younger, you'd be in big trouble right about now." She laughed a rough, smoky laugh. She reminded him so much of Lucille Ball, the actress, whose old shows he remembered watching as a kid. Stella was such a character, with vibrant, dyed red hair and a round face that was always heavily painted, with thick mile-long lashes he was pretty sure were fake. Neil dropped the plush towel on the lounge chair before sprawling in it to finish drying off in his dark bathing trunks.

"Listen, Neil, I wanted to talk to you about Candy." Stella sat in the olive green padded chair beside him and shoved on a pair of dark sunglasses, her lips coated with a vibrant red lipstick. She was quite the package, trademark Stella, a transplanted Canadian from the prairie province of Manitoba. She'd moved here with her husband twenty years before. He'd since died, but she had flourished and become as much a part of this paradise as the white sandy beaches that dotted the shoreline.

"Well, I'd rather not." Neil smiled as he shut his eyes, but unfortunately it was Candy's sweet face and slim curves, all that mile-long lush hair he dreamed of one day running his hands through, that popped up in his mind. He wiped his hand down his face and held back the growl that wanted to burst out.

"Oh, come on, Neil. Be nice."

"Nice, are you kidding me?" Neil was propelled forward by the frustration he'd been carrying around for Candy since she'd slapped his face earlier that morning. He slid his legs around the side and sat up, facing Stella. "I've been more than nice to her. Every time I see her, she wants nothing more than to claw my eyes out. What did I ever do to her? Seriously, Stella, I'm done with that chick. That girl has serious issues or something. I mean, what the hell is it with her, anyway? It's like she's got a poker jammed so far up her ass that she's..." Neil stopped talking as Stella slid her glasses down her nose with an expression of amusement. "What?" he snapped.

This was so unlike him. He was the reasonable Friessen, the one who smoothed things over, the negotiator. But, Candy McCrae had the ability to turn him into one of those rough, uncivilized alphas like his brother Jed and, at times, Brad, who barked and growled and stalked around like cavemen. Their wives just shook their heads because there was no reasoning with them. Neil had always laughed and tried to lighten the moment, but it was no fun when it was him and his reasoning that had hit the road all because of a woman.

"Neil, Candy is a very nice young lady. You just don't know her, and..." She held up her hand and reached out to touch Neil's when he nearly lost it, waving his hand in the air like a madman. "She's in trouble. I am cautious about saying this because of how she covets her privacy, but I can't stand by anymore on the sideline. She's out there all alone with those damn horses, and did you know she rescued a baby donkey two weeks ago? As if she needs another mouth to feed. Its mother was killed, and she's been feeding it from a bottle, nursing the thing just like a baby. The first two days, she barely had any sleep. Francisco told me that. Apparently, she went to him. She didn't know what to feed the animal, and she was absolutely exhausted when he stopped in to see how she was coping. She does things like that, you know." She raised her eyebrows at him as if he didn't have a clue.

"Francisco came to see me this morning about Candy," Neil said. "You know how he is. He never butts in on anyone's business, but he told me Candy went to him and asked him to partner with her in her land, that she'd sell him a share. He wouldn't tell me how much, just that it was too low and he couldn't let her do that. He doesn't have much, and she knew that, too, but apparently she was willing to take very little. He said she's in a bad way." Neil realized he had little hope of getting Candy out of his head any time soon, especially with the way Stella was watching him, as if she could read his mind and discern how he really felt about Candy. "I went to see her this morning. She damn near clawed out my eyes, Stella. I tried to offer her money and partner with her on that property, but she wouldn't even hear an offer, not from me."

"Hmm, well, I don't know what to tell you, Neil, but if you could try again, she really does need the help and I can't carry her much longer. She'll lose everything, and she doesn't deserve that fate. She's selling off her horses, too. Thought you should know that."

"Her gray one?" Neil hated to see her part with that big guy, but he wondered if maybe he could offer to buy her horses...if she was selling them.

"No, she loves Sable. Her dad gave her that Azteca. He's worth a pretty penny, too. I think she'd go to her grave first before parting with him. No, it's the other two." Stella pushed herself from the chair. "Now think about it. Go talk to her again, but don't tell her I came to see you. Work that slick charm of yours. Sweet-talk her. I know you can do it." Stella blew him a kiss and stalked away, her heels clicking on the concrete patio, her hips swaying as she tossed him a wave over her shoulder.

Neil picked up his towel and then tossed it back on the lounger. Sweet-talking and Candy were two things that never happened together, more like flares and shotguns.

"Aww," he groaned and swiped his hand over his face, because although he'd like nothing more than to turn his back on Candy and never speak to her again, he couldn't. Somehow, that sultry, sexy siren had found her way under his skin. Neil needed to find a way to convince Candy she needed him, and that would be an entire project in itself.

FOUR

Neil pressed his hand against the frame of the large floor-to-ceiling window in his comfortable living room, decorated in browns and greens. Everything outside was swaying, the palm trees, the bushes, his flag pole, a little too much for his liking.

"Mister Friessen, sir, the weather reports are saying the hurricane is two days out. They're ordering an evacuation, sir," Ana said. She was a short, plump Mayan in her early fifties who lived in a small cottage in back with her husband, Carlos. Ana looked after the house, and Carlos took care of the gardens, the maintenance, and all the upkeep required for a property of this size.

"Could be closer than that, Ana." He could feel Ana standing just inside the entryway, and he knew she and Carlos would stay behind and take care of everything if he let them.

"Do you think it will miss us, sir? Carlos said the last five have veered off in another direction at the last moment. Could happen again. Maybe it will be all right,"

Ana said, trying to sound hopeful, though Neil could hear the worry in her voice.

"I don't know, Ana. I think we need to get these windows boarded up, haul out all the storm shutters, seal this place up. But I think this time, maybe you and Carlos should head into Merida. Take the Jeep." Neil pushed away from the window and listened to the radio announce a yellow alert. He slid his hand over his scratchy jaw. He needed to shave, get cleaned up. Normally, he'd never walk around like this, but he had other things to worry about. Since the green alert had been issued a few hours before, he'd been waiting and watching.

"Okay, Ana, I want you two to get ready. It's too close. Call Carlos. I'm going to need his help to board up, and then I want both of you out of here." Neil pulled out a pair of boots from the closet and listened to Ana hurry away and shout out the door to Carlos. Then the phone rang. He knew who it was before Ana reappeared, holding the cordless handset.

"Mister Friessen, it's your father." Ana passed him the phone.

"Dad, how're Diana and the baby?"

"Wonderful! She's home now. We're just waiting for Jed and Diana to pick a name for this big boy. Your mother took a ton of pictures. But that's not why I'm calling. We've been following the news. You need to get out, son, and Ana and Carlos, too, before the hurricane makes it impossible," Rodney Friessen said from the other end of the line.

"I know. They just issued another warning a few minutes ago. I'm going to get everything boarded up, batten down the hatches. I'm sending Ana and Carlos out. I'll be right behind them after I make sure all the staff are gone," Neil said.

"Don't wait too long, and call us when you leave. I

want to know you're out of there. Your mother, you know how she is, she's already worrying."

Neil grabbed the boots he'd just pulled from the closet and sat down, jamming his feet into them as he sandwiched the phone between his shoulder and ear. "Well, it's your job to get Mom to stop worrying. Just tell her I'll be out of here soon. But I need to get going, Dad, so I can get everything boarded up."

"Okay, son. Take care, and remember to call as soon as you're out."

Neil tossed the disconnected phone on the desk and started out the front door to where Carlos and Raphael, a younger man who occasionally helped Carlos out, were securing boards over the windows. "We need to hurry, Carlos. The second alert was just issued, and the wind is starting to pick up."

"Sir, we drained the pool, and Raphael has already stored all the outdoor furniture in the shed and secured it."

"Sir, you have another call." Ana opened the front door and waved the phone she gripped in her hand.

Neil stuck a couple screws in the side of his mouth and lifted another board over one of the other windows. "If that's my dad again, I'll call him later," Neil mumbled as he fingered another of the shiny screws from his mouth and screwed it into the wood.

"Sir, it's not your dad. It's Miss Stella," Ana shouted.

"I'll call her back, Ana. I don't have time to talk to her right now," Neil snapped, because he realized he was supposed to go see Candy yesterday and he hadn't. He was still humiliated and didn't have a clue how to deal with that prickly woman.

"I'll tell her." Ana disappeared back in the house but then reappeared a second later, right behind Neil, holding the phone out. He could hear Stella shouting and carrying on as Ana walked the phone to him. "She don't want to hear it, and she said something nasty I can't repeat and told me to get you on the phone."

"Oh, for the love of God." Neil passed the cordless drill to Ana and took the phone.

"Stella, I'll call you back. I need to get the windows boarded. We're kind of in a hurry here. In case you haven't noticed, we've got a storm coming in."

"No, you can't call me back. Did you go see Candy yesterday like you told me you would?" She sounded really irritated on the other end.

"I'm sorry, I didn't have a chance. Listen, I'll deal with it after this storm passes. I'll sit her down and have a talk with her, but now is not the time. Everyone's evacuating, and I hope you are, too."

"I'm leaving now, but I can't get a hold of Candy. You and I both know, Neil, that she won't leave her place. She won't leave those damn animals, and how is she going to move them? She hasn't got a dime to her name, or have you forgotten our conversation?" Stella barked, and he was positive that if she were standing before him, he'd feel the heat of her fury as she took another strip off him.

"She's a big girl, Stella. I'm sure she can take care of herself." Neil couldn't believe he'd said that, and obviously neither could Stella, because he listened to silence from the other end for what felt like precious seconds, time he didn't have to spare right now, and then she let out a heavy sigh.

"Neil Friessen, you surprise me. I never took you for someone who'd turn his back on someone else. All I'm asking is for you to go out there. If she hasn't left, convince her to leave. Hell, toss her over those big, broad shoulders and carry her out of there if she won't listen."

Maybe it was the worry he picked up in Stella's voice, and her heavy sigh, that had him softening and going against his better judgement. "Fine, I'll go out there. I'll check to see if she's still there. I'll do it on my way out. But I can't force her—"

Stella cut him off. "Neil, just talk to her. Don't take no for an answer. Please get her out of there, because you and I both know she won't leave. She probably turned off her radio and isn't even listening to it."

Neil banged the phone to his forehead. "Fine. If she's still there, I'll handle it. Now I've got to go, Stella. Make sure you leave now."

"On my way out the door. Thank you, thank you, you big hunk of man."

Stella hung up, and Neil handed Ana the phone. For a minute, as Ana watched him in a way his mother often did, Neil wondered if she had read his mind.

"Come on, let's finish." Neil grabbed another sheet of wood and glanced out at the swaying trees. He felt that something different was coming this way, something he couldn't put his finger on about this storm, this hurricane, that he knew would change everything.

CHAPTER
FIVE

Candy's phone had long since gone dead. She'd lost power hours ago. Her house, although sheltered by trees, was right on the ocean and directly in the path of this storm. She'd listened to the radio and heard the first warning, the green one. She hadn't worried then, but when she heard the second warning, yellow alert, she started to move her horses to the adobe barn they used only during bad weather and the few times of the year when the rains were heavy and unpredictable. That barn was far back in the trees at the far edge of her property, the piece that backed onto the Friessen parcel. It was sheltered and hard to get to, and Candy had to haul everything by hand. With the water, the hay, and the feed, it took all day and a lot of work every time they were forced to take shelter.

Today, as she hauled bucket after bucket of water to the barn, the muscles in her arms burned, and she'd swear her thighs were about to give out under the weight she carried, over and over, back and forth. Typically, she could have used the quad with the small trailer attached, but the quad had broken down months ago. She'd bought it second hand from a local farmer the year before, and the thing had been held together with duct tape and twine ever since.

She could hear Ambrose carrying on something awful from the house as she hurried back to the well with the empty buckets. He had to be terrified by the sounds of the storm pounding the ocean and whipping the rain and trees around them into an awful racket. Rain was pouring down in buckets, and with the wind gusting and picking up speed, shutting the baby donkey in her bedroom had been her only option. It was getting too dangerous out there for him. Even the horses had been spooking and freaking out until she moved them into the barn. Each time she lugged a bucket of water, filling the buckets in their stalls and the large extra wooden one just inside the barn, the horses snorted and neighed, and she could feel how tightly they were wound. She stayed out of their stalls and prayed this storm would veer away, changing course as so many others had done year after year.

She dropped the buckets and headed back down the path, jogging and stumbling through the puddles and mud, trying to figure out how she'd haul those heavy bales of hay all this way by hand. Then she tripped and fell. "Oh my God!" She groaned from the pain shooting up her back, straining her shoulders as she pushed her way up on her knees. Candy was used to hard work, but this was beyond anything she'd done in a long time. She didn't know how she'd continue, but she knew that if she didn't hurry, they'd be in real trouble. She heard a smack and bang, the sound of the horses whinnying and screaming, and she glanced back at the adobe barn and realized the wind was shooting through the open windows. She hurried back as the palomino started to carry on, making a horrible, terrified sound, kicking and banging at the walls.

Candy raced around the outside to where one of the shutters had been torn off and was dangling by a hinge. She needed to get a hammer and nails quickly, so she started running down the path, soaked by the rain that was pouring down, and could hear her panicked donkey in the house. Something crashed and shattered inside, but she couldn't stop and worry about what it was, and she couldn't take him out just yet. For now, he'd be safe, but not her stuff, her things. She sighed. Every crash meant she was losing a piece from the Johnson Brothers Friendly Village china set. She'd fallen in love with the pattern and scraped together every dime she had to buy the outrageously expensive pieces, and not once had she ever used them. But it was just stuff; there was no contest between things, and her animals. Items could be replaced, but her animals were living and breathing creatures whom she loved deeply.

She gasped for breath as she slid the bar off the shed where the hay was stored. She wanted to take a minute and rest before she fell down, as she'd been at this for hours, running on pure adrenaline, soaked from sweat and rain. She remembered the hammer and nails she needed to secure the shutters on the barn to keep out the wind so she could calm her horses down. They were on the porch with her tools, just inside the door. She held her side as she raced to the small squared-in porch. She grabbed the hammer, shoved a handful of nails into her front pocket, and then lifted her rain coat and pulled it on over her wet shirt. She stepped off the porch and into a puddle, her wet socks sloshing inside her hiking boots as she ran back to the shed.

Candy knew she wouldn't be able to make too many

trips with the hay. As she lifted off the board that secured the door and dumped it on the ground, she stumbled under the weight. She was so tired; her arms ached, she was shivering from being so wet, and the wind was showing no mercy. Her legs trembled as she staggered inside and spotted the old wheelbarrow leaning against the wooden wall, which had so many cracks that the wind was whistling through it. "Stupid Candy, you could have used this for the buckets." She wanted to kick herself in the ass; she could have made more trips, saved her energy, if she'd taken the wheelbarrow the first time. She cursed and grabbed it, setting it beside her so she could load in the bales of hay. She figured she could get two on top and balance another on the handle, and maybe that would be enough for a couple of days. That was all she needed to get through, she thought, until the gusts of this hurricane blew past, and then she could come back and get some more.

There were only two bales left on the ground, but she'd need to stand on one to reach the top bale from the next stacked row. Her pitchfork, where the hell was her pitchfork? She couldn't remember where she'd left it, and she needed it to hook into the top bales and pull them down. Dammit, she'd have to stack another bale on top of the one just to reach the string. She lifted the heavy bale, set it on top, and climbed up, stretching to reach that top bale. She was on her tiptoes, and almost had the twine at the tip of her finger. She stretched a little more and finally slipped her finger under the tight twine and yanked toward her again and again, and it started tumbling forward along with another bale. She tried to hold back the second bale, but it was too heavy, and she felt herself going backward, off balance. She hit the ground, landing on her side, two bales slamming into her chest. Her breath whooshed out from the force of the blow. It took a second, a minute, of stunned silence as she lay with her leg twisted until she wondered what had happened.

She blinked in the dim light as she listened to a braying in the distance, the rattle of shutters banging, the whistle of the wind and rain pounding the old roof. Candy shoved at the bale, but her arms gave out, now nothing more than limp noodles. She had not an ounce of strength, and she couldn't stop the flood of tears and the sob that racked her body as she lay there, helpless, and fell apart.

CHAPTER
SIX

Neil leaned into the four-door covered Jeep as Ana fastened her seatbelt and Carlos started the vehicle, their suitcases piled in back. "Go now. Don't wait for me."

"Sir, we'll follow you to Miss Candy's...."

Neil cut off Carlos because the rain was pummelling them and the wind was so strong he could feel it beating against the slicker he'd pulled on while helping load up the Jeep. "No, you're not waiting. I want you out of here now. I'm right behind you. I'll stop at Candy's and pick her up. We won't be far behind you. Now go." He slapped the roof of the Jeep and slammed the door. Neil had already loaded up his SUV with an overnight bag and some supplies, food, and water, which Ana had put together for all of them. "Just in case" was what she had said, but then, by the looks of things, with the red alert having gone out a while ago and the storm uninterested in veering past them, it had been a really good idea. Neil just hoped the damage wouldn't be too bad and the roads out wouldn't be too jammed with traffic.

Neil followed the taillights of the Jeep down the long, winding driveway to the narrow road. Wipers scraped the windshield, barely keeping the rain off. Branches, leaves, and other blowing debris smacked the car. It was becoming really hard to see. "Come on, Carlos. Easy does it." Neil had to keep a tight grip on the steering wheel, so he really hoped Carlos could get himself and Ana out quickly and stay on the road.

Ahead, Carlos turned left, which would lead to the highway. Neil turned right and headed down the narrow rutted road that led to Candy's. He'd stop, and, God forbid, if the woman was still there, he'd toss her in the passenger seat and drive. "Yeah, right, studly. As if she's going to allow you to set your hooks in her." He'd beg if he had to, but he was getting ahead of himself. Candy had probably already left, of course. It would be insane to stay out there all alone. There had to be some sort of common sense in that stubborn, gorgeous head. "Oh, great." Neil snorted as he realized, pulling in beside her small adobe and spotting her old truck parked right beside it, that the damn stubborn, pigheaded woman was still there.

"Work the charm, Neil." He stepped out into the blowing wind, shutters smacking, an awful braying coming from inside the house, and yelled, "Candy!"

There was nothing.

CHAPTER
SEVEN

She heard a vehicle, its tires splashing through the puddles, then a car door shutting. She lay on her side with a bale on her legs and another on her chest, the hay tickling her nose. She pushed and shoved harder, rolling further onto her side to slide out from under them. Something sharp and painful poked into her outer thigh, her hip, and she yelled. Then she heard Neil shout out her name. He could be loud when he wanted to be, and Candy, for the first time ever, wanted to weep from the sound of his voice. It was so welcome and soothing. This was the "knight in shining armor" feeling that everyone talked about, that books were written about, but she had never understood what it was until now.

She crawled on her knees, dragging her one leg against the sharp pinch from each jolting movement, into the rain, the wind, and over the muddy ground, her hands sliding through the mucky puddles. "Neil!" she called out. Her voice squeaked from the throbbing in her leg.

She tried to look around but had to squint. The rain

pelting down and the wind gusting made it impossible to
see anything clearly. She spotted a fancy black SUV, one of
the Friessen vehicles, one she'd seen Neil drive many times,
but she didn't see him now. She didn't know where he was.
"Neil, I'm here! Please help me!" she cried again. She tried
to stand, but something pinched her left leg right below her
hip bone, and it hurt like hell. It was better to keep it bent
beneath her and drag it along, and then the throbbing
wouldn't be so bad.

"Candy!"

She heard him yell again and squinted to where she
could see him coming out of her house. He was on the
front step, looking around for her. She raised her hand up
as she balanced on her knee, her left side shaky. Every time
she moved, it hurt like a burning fire shooting shards of
glass into her leg. Instead of getting better, it was worse.
"Neil!" she cried out again. This time, she knew he saw
her, because he was running toward her.

"What did you do? Why are you still here?" he yelled.
He was on the ground, kneeling in front of her in the mud,
in the puddles, the rain running off his dark shell jacket.

She couldn't help herself as she started crying again,
clinging to the arm he slid around her. Neil made it so easy
then, as he pulled her against his chest, his arms holding
her, and, for a moment, she felt safe.

He slid his hand around the back of her head, into her
wet, tangled hair. "Come on. We have to get out of here."
He slid his hand under her arm to help her up. "Did you
hurt yourself? Candy, talk to me." His face was so close to
hers, leaning in toward her. She could smell his minty
breath, and she welcomed the warmth.

She held on to the sleeve of his jacket. "I was trying to
get the hay to my horses. I lost my balance, and two bales
fell, knocked me over, and landed on me. My leg, my thigh,

it hurts here at the joint, where my hip is." She stuttered as she slid her hand down to her hip, and Neil's hand instantly covered hers.

"Okay, I'm going to lift you, get you out of the rain, so I can take a look." He slid his arm around her waist to help her up.

"Oh, crap, Neil, that hurts," she cried as she kept her hand on her leg, just below her hip, and realized then as she felt the bumps in her pocket, and the sharp poke from the nails, what was causing the pain.

"I know, Candy." He had her in his arms and carried her into the shed she'd crawled from minutes ago. He kicked a bale of hay and set her on it, laying her on her side. "Show me again where it hurts." He was kneeling in front of her.

"Right here. I had nails in my pocket and a hammer, too. I think it might be a nail."

"The hammer's here on the ground." Neil shoved her hand away from her leg. "You're bleeding right below your hip, Candy. I have to take your pants down to get a better look."

She nodded. "I can't straighten it out. It hurts too much."

"I'm going to do this slowly, but I have to put my hands on you, okay?" He held them up for a moment as if he needed her permission, and she saw his hesitation, as if he thought she might freak out and scream if he touched her. But then, she'd given him plenty of reason, even though the truth was that her body craved his touch.

He pulled back his hood on his dark slicker, and he had such confidence in his eyes, just a spark of which she would have killed for. He was here, Neil was here for her, and because of that, she couldn't find her voice. It was lodged deep somewhere between her shame, her worry, and her desire for him.

"Candy." He touched her arm, leaned over her.

"Okay, just do it." She choked it out.

Neil untied the drawstring and pulled down the zipper. He slipped his hand inside her pants and started to pull them down, and she felt the sharp shooting pain as if a hot poker were ramming into her leg. She grabbed his wrist.

"Candy, you've got a nail in your leg, right below your pelvis. Jesus, Candy, what were you doing?" Neil snapped, and she could feel how tense he was as he glanced over his shoulder at the rain and branches blowing. The storm had picked up.

"Neil, pull it out, please. It's one of the nails from my pocket. I need to nail down the shutters on the barn where I put the horses. I have to hurry. I was trying to move the hay. Please help me. It's the only way I can get them to stop freaking out and keep some of the storm out." She squeezed his wrist harder as he slid it inside her pants and along her hip.

"This is going to hurt, Candy. I'd rather get you help, a hospital, a clinic, find a doctor somewhere."

"No!" she yelled, then pounded her fist into his chest, but he grabbed it and held both her hands before she could swing again. He watched her, but his expression was filled with fury and stubbornness, something so solid that she knew he was thinking of scooping her up and tossing her into his vehicle. There was something else there, too, and she hoped she wasn't wrong, because right now she needed him.

"Please, Neil, my horses. My baby donkey is in the house. I can't leave them. Just take out the nail and go. I'm not going to any hospital. I have to get the hay to my horses. They were freaking out from the wind when I left. I need to nail the old shutters closed. They were hanging, and...I have to protect my—my horses." She was shaking and couldn't stop the stutter. She was just so cold, or maybe it was from shock. She didn't know for sure anymore. She was tired, too.

Neil's expression became hard and unreadable. He glanced away and shook his head. When he looked back at her, his lips were a fine white line. "Dammit, Candy, you are the most stubborn, pigheaded woman, and if you think I'm going to just leave you here, you don't know me very well." Neil slid his hand over her hip, inside her pants, and she could feel when the cloth pulled at the nail. "This could be really deep, Candy, and I don't know what you've nicked. Could be an artery or a vein. This is stupid and dangerous."

He yanked hard, and Candy screamed. She didn't know how he had done it, but he had her pants down to her knees and was pressing his hand over the puncture, holding it so it didn't hurt as much.

"It's bleeding quite a bit, Candy. I need to wrap it."

She didn't have a chance to say a word as he scooped her up in his arms and carried her into the wind-driven rain, fighting against it as he staggered with her to the house.

Candy could hear Ambrose braying and banging something in her bedroom, and Neil set her on the old sofa. "I'll be right back."

She watched him as he moved away from her toward her tiny, boxlike bathroom. Neil was tall, and this house seemed to crowd him.

"Candy, do you have any antibiotic cream, anything for cuts? And why the hell is there a donkey in the house?"

"There's some alcohol and iodine, I think, in the cabinet under the sink." She giggled, but it wasn't rational at all. "I couldn't leave Ambrose outside. It's safer in here."

She could hear Neil rummaging, and he reappeared a few seconds later with towels and two plastic bottles, one of alcohol, the other iodine, but she realized that one was probably empty.

"You named your donkey Ambrose?"

He set the towels beside her and she felt herself warm as she realized she was in only her thin panties, that were wet and sheer, and he could see everything. Neil pulled up a stool and sat down scooting a towel under her leg and slid it up to where blood dribbled from where the nail had been. A bad spot right below her hip bone at the joint to her leg. And she stared at the ugly puncture the burning ache started building, and it hurt like hell. And she worried for a minute of bacteria and whatever else was on that nail, and the oozing puncture.

"This is going to hurt." Neil said as he unscrewed the white bottle.

Candy toed off her wet boot, more for something to do, as she turned her head away and pressed the back of her wrist over her eyes. "Please just do it fast." She felt sick, anticipating, waiting. She could feel every movement Neil made. His arm brushed her bare thigh, and she was so aware of her indecency that it was absolutely embarrassingly awkward, having her pants down around her knees.

He pressed his arm across her chest to give her something to hold on to as he poured, and the burning, ripping sting hit fast and hard as the cold, clear alcohol sizzled over the wound. She tried to stifle her scream as he pressed a towel against it and fresh blood dribbled out.

"I'm going to be sick." She was shaking, and perspiration was beading her forehead as the nausea rolled in her stomach. The room started spinning as she slapped her hand over her mouth and bolted upright, and Neil scooped her up in his arms as if she weighed nothing. He had her at the toilet in a second, and what made it worse was that he was lifting her hair back so she wouldn't get puke splattered in it. It was such an intimate, caring gesture. As his arm secured her so she wouldn't fall on legs that were ready to give out, she retched and retched. The throbbing in the other leg was just beginning to subside from something ugly to just an annoying ache that would keep her awake.

She spit and wiped her shaking hand over her mouth.

"Do you have fresh water?" Neil asked as he helped her sit on the floor.

Candy pointed with her shaky hand toward the small kitchen, where a plastic jug of water sat on the counter. He must have understood, as he let her sit on the floor in just her underwear and camisole top, her pants having been lost along the way.

He was back moments later with a cup of water and kneeling down in front of her. "Here, drink this."

Her hand was shaking, and he held the cup to her lips as she swallowed the warm water. She wiped the water dribbling from the side of her mouth with the back of her hand.

"Better?" he asked.

She nodded. "Yes, sorry, I—I..."

He cut her off with a sharp nod and scooped her back in his arms, carrying her to the sofa. It was over far too soon: His arms were gone from around her, and she mourned the loss. There was something about the security of his arms that she wanted so badly but also feared more than anything. He laid her back on the old battered green sofa. "I need to get this covered. Do you have any bandages, gauze?"

"No." It was one of those essentials that was on the "not necessary" list, but she definitely wasn't telling Neil that.

Neil didn't wait; he ripped one of the towels into strips, wrapped them around her leg, and knotted the ends. "This is going to have to do." He glanced around, and she could see he was worried. Bloody hell, so was she, but she needed to get to the horses before they completely freaked out. He grabbed her wet pants from the floor. "Do you have a dry pair...?"

Ambrose interrupted by braying and banging her door.

"I've got to get him! He's going to hurt himself." Candy started to get up. "Help me up, please, Neil."

"Candy, you need to listen to me. We have to go now. There's a hurricane coming in. We can't stay here, it's not safe. It's going to be hard to get out of here now." He held her cheeks between both his hands and conveyed to her how serious he was with the power of his amber eyes. All the light teasing that she had always chalked up to nothing serious, just him looking for a good time, was gone, replaced with an expression that let her know he meant what he was saying. It was something so solid she could lean on it, and any other time, she would maybe have liked it. No, she would have loved it. But not now.

Candy winced as she swung her leg over the side of the sofa. "I have dry pants in my drawer. But I have to take care of my horses."

Neil left her sitting there and hurried down the hall, toward the kicking and braying. He burst into her room and shouted at Ambrose, then kicked the door closed behind him.

"Bottom drawer, Neil," Candy shouted as she listened to him open and close drawers, not that she had many in her rickety four-drawer dresser.

He returned seconds later clutching a skirt, one of her longer paisley ones. He was shaking his head. "You'll never get those skinny jeans on with that towel around your leg." He held her skirt out and helped her dress as if she were two years old. He picked up her soaking wet boot and dropped it. "You have rubber boots?"

Candy pointed. "Back door."

Neil was gone, returning a second later with a pair of old gumboots. "Put these on. We're leaving now. I'll get the donkey."

"Unless you're planning on taking my horses, too, I'm not going anywhere." She crossed her arms and tried to stand, but her trembling, shaking leg gave out.

He jammed his hands in his short wet hair and seemed to pull as if she were driving him crazy. "Candy, we're not staying."

The wind rattled the door, and branches whacked the side of the house. She couldn't see through the tears that glossed over her eyes as she stared up at the one man who had kept her awake night after night for so long. She hated him, but her body and heart told her a different story. He was standing here before her, and he wasn't leaving.

His face softened. "Where're the nails?"

"There's a box at the back door." This time, she managed to stand and follow him, pressing her hand over the towel, which eased the ache as she moved, dragging her leg behind her.

Neil grabbed a handful of nails and shoved them into his coat pocket. "Stay here. I'll be right back." He yanked up his hood and pushed open the door, shutting it behind him.

Candy hurried to the window, afraid it would shatter, and watched Neil struggle against the wind to the shed. He reappeared seconds later, running down the trail toward the barn. That was when Ambrose let out a screech and brayed, kicking at something, and she heard a splinter and a crash. She sighed.

"Coming, Ambrose. I'm coming." She hobbled to her bedroom, for the first time worrying about Neil and willing him to hurry back.

EIGHT

"They were gone." Neil was soaking wet and out of breath by the time he yanked open the door and had to use both hands to pull it closed as the wind whipped around. "Candy, we're leaving now, if we can still get out of here."

"What do you mean, 'They were gone'? They can't be gone!" she yelled, and Neil watched as her face took on that pasty gray white that happened to people when they heard the most awful news. She was holding that ridiculous floppy-eared donkey in her lap, with its gangly legs, as she sat awkwardly on a stool by the door.

Of course she wasn't going to make this easy. She was going to be difficult as all hell. He'd love to get to know this woman, and at any other time he would have enjoyed sparring a few rounds, except now was about the worst time possible. Neil took two steps toward her until he was right in her face and the donkey's legs knocked his knees. He grabbed her shoulders and put his face inches from hers. "You listen to me: Those horses were probably damn scared, and it looks like they kicked out those flimsy stall doors. There wasn't much there to hold them in. We have to go."

"No. I'll go find them...."

"No, you won't. They'll be miles from here by now. Candy, honey, I know you love them, but animals have a sixth sense about this kind of thing. They'll get the hell out of here, they'll run. You know they're prey animals, built with a fight or flight instinct that appears to have completely missed you. We have to go. Come on. Don't fight me on this, because I'll make you go, and you know I can. I'm not leaving you here. Candy, I promise you we'll find them after. I'll help you find them!" he yelled at her.

The wind was ripping at the roof. The metal was screeching and banging, and water was dribbling through the roof as new holes seemed to pop up everywhere. Her entire ceiling now resembled a sieve. The floor was wet, and Neil could feel the way the house wanted to buckle around them. It wouldn't be standing much longer.

A tear slipped out, and she couldn't wipe it away. He could tell she was embarrassed, but her hands were full with that stupid, ridiculous donkey, who was looking up at Neil absolutely petrified. He could see the thing quivering.

"I have goats' milk in the fridge for Ambrose. We'll have to take it."

Neil didn't wait, yanking open the fridge door. There were five bottles of milk in the fridge, and he grabbed all of them. Spotting paper bags stuffed in a cubby, he stuffed all the bottles in. "Let's go now. Give me the donkey." He lifted the donkey from Candy, and it started braying and kicking. He held on tightly to it and to the paper bag he scrunched in his hand. "Can you walk?"

"Yeah, I can...."

"Hang on to me."

She slid her hand into the crook of his arm, and Neil

walked to the door. The donkey had calmed down, thankfully. He adjusted the bag in his hand so he could open the door, but he could feel the wind pounding and pushing against it.

"Don't let go." He glanced back for a second as she tightened her grip, pressing right up against him.

As soon as he turned that knob, the door blew out of his hands and smacked into the wall, nearly knocking him off his feet. He yelled back to Candy, "Hang on," as he moved toward his SUV, leaning into the wind, which had such force that it was a battle for him to stay upright. He pulled Candy along to his SUV, which was rattling and shaking as if the wind were going to pick it up any second. Candy stumbled and went down. Neil didn't know how, but he scooped her under his arm and dragged her with the bag and the donkey. He pressed her against the SUV and opened the passenger door, and she jumped in. Neil dumped the donkey on her lap, the bag at her feet, and had to lean against the door to shove it closed.

A huge gust blew into him, knocking him down. He stumbled to his feet and had to crouch against the wind to get around to the driver's side. They weren't getting a break, and he wondered whether they'd missed the small window to get out. He could feel a fury whipping all around him as if it were trapping them there, and for the first time ever, he worried about whether they'd find a way to get to shelter, to get to safety.

He struggled to open his door, sliding under the wheel, and used both hands to pull the door closed. His key dangled from the ignition, and he turned it, starting the engine the first time. He jammed his foot on the gas pedal, spinning the wheels and his Tahoe around, driving back the way he had come.

"Jesus, Neil, are we going to make it?" She cried out

when he skidded in the mud, the wind pushing his back end around. The road was flooding, and the water was already up to the wheel wells, making it a nightmare to drive anywhere as fast as he needed to. Time was not on their side. Every second he had been at Candy's had lost them precious minutes, because once this storm had them in its clutches, there was little they could do to pull away.

"Get your seatbelt on, and hang on!" he yelled.

This was a hell of a ride, and he flinched as Candy screamed when a flying branch that resembled half a tree slammed into the windshield, cracking the glass just above her head. Then one of the gates to his estate ripped off its steel hinges and flew past the windshield.

"Neil, look out!" Candy screamed and grabbed his shoulder, her hand sliding out to protect him just as a tree toppled and fell in front of him. Neil swerved and slammed the brakes, skidding in the water and mud just as the tree hit the ground and the side of his SUV crashed into it.

"Shit!" he yelled, then swiped his hand over his face right before he shoved the car in reverse and backed up, scraping his side of the vehicle again.

"Neil, what are we going to do? How are we going to get around that tree?"

"We can't get around it." He shoved the gear in drive and cranked the wheel, turning them around.

"Neil, where are you going?" She sounded worried, Neil could hear it in her voice, but he also knew she wouldn't cry. She'd hold it together.

He squinted through the windshield, the wipers on the highest setting, whirring and doing little to keep off the rain that poured down in sheets. He struggled to see as he drove into the wind, the back end of the SUV spinning side to side as the wind tried to push them off what was left of the road. Then he saw it, the twin oaks at the side of the driveway. The remaining gate swung back and forth as water and mud sloshed around it, and he spun the steering wheel, turning down the driveway, hoping it would take them far enough away from the ugly claws of the surging storm. "We're going the only place we can, to my place."

CHAPTER
NINE

"What do you mean, your place?" she asked, and the donkey decided then to show them that he wasn't housebroken, as he emptied his bladder and a heap of dung on Candy's lap. "Oh, Ambrose, my skirt!"

The donkey leaned in toward Candy and appeared almost embarrassed, but Candy couldn't be mad at him, not Ambrose, not ever. He was cute, adorable, and he depended on her, even though he'd just dumped an awful, smelly mess all over her skirt.

Neil didn't appear to notice or care as tight lines creased across his forehead. He glanced back but seemed far too worried to be irritated by the ripe smell. Candy went to press the button to unroll the window and get some air.

"Don't you dare open that window. Leave it alone," he shouted as both his hands gripped the wheel.

"Sorry, I don't know what I was thinking." She slid her hand away from the door and back around Ambrose. When he tried to stand up and jabbed his hoof right beside the nail puncture, she swore she could see stars. "Ow!" she yelled at him and swatted his backside, making him sit back down.

"You okay?" Neil asked.

"Yeah. I'm so sorry, Neil," she said, because she was. This was her fault. If he hadn't come for her, he'd be long gone, somewhere safe, and he wouldn't be stuck with a vehicle that smelled like a barn.

He nodded. "Look, I got it, but I wasn't leaving you." He let out a heavy sigh. "Listen, we're going to have to ride it out here. We're stuck, Candy. We've got a better chance here at my place, hopefully it's structurally sound enough to withstand a hurricane."

He didn't glance her way, and she wasn't sure if he had said it for her benefit or his, because there had been a hesitation—she thought there had been, anyway. She couldn't help worrying that this was all her fault. He had come for her, and if he hadn't stayed to help her, if he hadn't gone to the barn for her horses, if he hadn't come for her at all, he'd be safe, yet here he was, doing everything he could for her. She understood that; she just didn't know why. There were easier ways to get a hold of her property other than putting himself in danger or getting himself killed. Candy had to pause for a moment as she tried to come to terms with that thought. She watched him gripping the wheel so hard that it appeared to bend, and she knew he was doing this for her, for her donkey. None of it made any sense.

"Neil, I'm so sorry. If it wasn't for me, you wouldn't be here in this...awful mess. Why did you come for me? Why did you stay?"

The glance he gave her was filled with something that confused her tired, frazzled mind, at the same time there was something else in his expression that terrified her in a way that she craved.

"You don't know? Seriously?" was all he said as he slammed his brakes in front of a large building. "Stay here." He was out the door, hunched over in the rain as the wind tried to blow him over, knock him down. She could tell it was taking all his effort, everything he had, to get to that door. The wipers were still working madly, and then he reappeared.

Ambrose was drooling over her arm, and she glanced down into his worried gray eyes. "It's okay, baby." She tried to soothe him by petting his side, holding him tighter. The door jerked open, and the wind gusted in with such force that Candy almost lost her grip on Ambrose. She couldn't see anything. As she gasped, Neil climbed back in and then struggled to pull the door closed.

"Bad idea, that was."

"What was a bad idea?" she asked, taking in the fact that he was dripping everywhere, his dark hair soaked and windblown, water all over his face.

"Parking in the garage. Listen, I'm pulling up to the back of the house. It won't be pretty, but there's no way I'll be able to get across the yard with you, let alone the donkey." Neil cranked the wheel and drove awfully fast, shoving hedges and bushes aside and steering the SUV as if it were a toy car. She didn't know how Neil managed to keep it going; it was swerving back and forth as he raced over what had once been green grass by the hedges and slammed on the brakes as he pulled up to the house, her side closest to the door.

"Neil, climb over me. Go out my side."

He shook his head as he shut off the engine. "No, I'll hurt you, and once your door opens, I need to have a hold of you. That wind is going to toss you as if you're nothing but a ragdoll. Stay put until I get you, until I get the door open, understand?" He meant every word he barked out to her. Although she loved to go head to head with him, she had no intention now of doing anything but listening. He started to open his door.

"Neil, please, I don't want you to get hurt."

Ambrose took that moment to panic and squirm, and his back hoof jammed Candy right where the puncture was at the juncture of her outer thigh, again. "Ow, dammit, dammit, Ambrose! Shit, that hurts."

Neil grabbed the donkey and shoved its head in his jacket as he pushed open his door. The wind whipped in, and Neil pressed his back to the door, leaning in with his entire body to shut it as he stumbled around the vehicle. How in the hell was he going to get to the door? Candy gripped the dashboard, watching in horror, awe, and amazement as he skidded, went down on his knees, and finally made it to the door, not once letting go of her donkey. She could see nothing now as the rain pounded the windows in sheets and buckets, so much fiercer than in a car wash. All she could see now was a blur.

"Dammit, Neil, please be okay." She lifted her skirt to dump some of the mess left by Ambrose onto the floor. She reached down to her feet and picked up the paper bag of milk, all she had for Ambrose. How was she going to get more? He was too young for anything else, and it was Francisco who'd given her the goats' milk. If he had left, how would she get more? Her heart ached as she thought of her horses, terrified and running wild in a warzone with no shelter, debris and trees and mud and water coming at them. She hoped Neil was right and they were far away from here, because her thoughts were taking her to some pretty dark places. She thought of her horses trapped, not knowing if they were dead or alive. *Please be okay.*

She scooted around on her seat, but her damn leg was going to be a problem, as it pinched and burned and hurt every time she moved. But if Neil could do it, so could she. She slid her fingers around the handle and pulled, but she wasn't prepared for the wind ripping the door right out and away from her hand. Somehow, she fell and felt herself being yanked and pulled from the wind, going down on her hands and knees, the bag underneath her, and she tried to grab hold of Neil's Tahoe, her fingers wrapping around the silver bar of the running board. Her hair was whipping around, she couldn't see, and then there were hands under her arms, pulling her against his solid chest and dragging her toward the door. She crawled inside and lay on the wet tiled floor as Neil somehow shut the door.

CHAPTER
TEN

"What the fuck were you doing? I told you very clearly to stay in the SUV. You almost got yourself killed. If I hadn't reached you, you would have been gone, blown across that yard. You scared the hell out of me, Candy!" he shouted at her as she sat on the floor, looking so vulnerable, and then she burst into tears. "Candy, ah, shit. Look, I'm sorry." He was down beside her, pulling off his wet jacket before lifting her in his arms and carrying her through the darkened house to the living room. She reeked, just like that ridiculous donkey he'd shut in the closet, but at least the thing was quiet now, for the moment, until he found a better spot, away from his shoes and coats.

She slid her arms around his neck and held on as he set her on the sofa. Then she started to get up. "Neil, I'm going to ruin this sofa. Ambrose peed on me, and there's dung ground into my skirt."

Neil stood her up and slid her skirt down, pulling off her wet jacket. "Take it off. I'll get you cleaned up in a minute. I want to check that wound, too. How's it feeling right now?"

He sat her back down in her sheer underwear and tank top, and she felt as if she were butt naked. She was blushing furiously, so he grabbed a blanket on the back of the sofa pulled it over her. She was trembling, and he thought this was because she was so upset, but then realized she was chilled because everything she wore was soaking wet. Her light tank top clung to her, and her hair dripped just like his.

"Let me get a towel. I'll be right back."

He left her shivering, perched on the side of the leather sofa, in a room that wasn't the safest place to be. He stopped for a second to get his head together. He knew he needed a plan B, whatever that hell that would be, because right now he was making everything up as he went along, and that wasn't a good thing. Right now was nowhere near as bad as things could get. They would need to ride out a storm that wasn't going to miss them, dodge them, or be another close call. It was coming right for them.

He grabbed an armful of towels from the laundry room and spotted a load of clothes folded on the side counter: his t-shirts, a sweatshirt. He dropped his wet coat on the floor and yanked off his wet shirt, buttons flying. He didn't have time to try to finger the buttons through the wet holes. He pulled on a t-shirt and grabbed one for Candy, as well as the sweatshirt, and hurried back. He dumped the bundle beside her on the sofa and took one look at her pasty face. She was shivering and didn't look good.

"I need to get you dry, Candy. Take off your wet shirt."

She jerked her head, and her teeth chattered. "Just don't look, please, Neil."

At any other time, he would have burst out laughing at

her modesty, but then it dawned on him, with the way she blushed, the way she tried to cover herself, that she was damn uncomfortable with her body, too innocent. He wondered for a minute if it was possible. Why had he not realized until now?

"I won't look. Come on." She dropped the blanket wrapped around her shoulders and fumbled with the hem of her tank top lifting it over her head and tossed the wet, sopping cloth on the floor. Her lacy bra was the same sheer fabric as her underwear, and dark nipples puckered against them.

"Bra too, Candy. I'm sorry, but it's wet." Her fingers shook as she reached back and unhooked it. The latch was stuck, and she had to pull a couple times until she freed it tossing the bra to the floor with her wet top. She crossed her arms over the most perfect, round, creamy breasts he'd ever seen.

He grabbed a towel and dried her and then her hair, then shoved one of his shirts over her head, lifting her heaps of wet tangled hair with his hand. Candy pulled the shirt over her breasts and down. Neil ran the towel again over her wet hair, squeezing out as much water as he could, and Candy lifted the blanket pooled around her waist as she shivered back over her shoulders, her teeth chattering as she trembled.

"I need some light. I need to get a look at your leg. Does it hurt?"

"Just a bit," she said in a way that was awfully quick.

He glanced at the shadows under her eyes. By how tight her face was, he knew it hurt a lot more than she said. He lifted the blanket covering the ripped towel he had tied around the puncture, but he realized it had shifted and now smelled of urine. He tried to untie it, but it was impossible. "Candy, I need to clean it again. I'll be right back."

He wasn't sure if she was shivering or nodding as she clutched the blanket across her chest and hunched forward. Neil hurried down the darkened hallway and didn't take long to gather what he needed: scissors, a flashlight, a first aid kid, and bottled water from the kitchen cupboard. Candy was lying down on the stiff leather, shivering, when he returned.

He dragged the sofa table over and set everything on it, kneeling beside her on the floor. "Candy, talk to me."

"Neil, I'm not feeling so good."

"Are you going to be sick again?"

He watched her dark eyes reach out to him, and she appeared to think about it and then shook her head. "I'll be okay, I'm just aching," she said.

Neil moved the blanket that covered her leg and cut off the sopping towel. He sniffed the ammonia from the animal and worried that it had seeped into the wound. Along with the dirty nail, he worried that rust could have found a way into her bloodstream. He wasn't a doctor, but he knew enough about infections like this to understand that it could escalate quickly into something serious. "Tetanus shots up to date?" he asked her.

Her eyes, which hadn't left his face, widened, and she shook her head.

"Of course they wouldn't be," he said. "I mean, living way out here, having your shots up to date would make you reasonable, a problem solver, someone who avoided risk, and you'd have made sure you were a long way away from here before this storm came close. So no surprise." He knew he was venting, but he couldn't help it. This woman, in the last few hours, had caused him more worry than he had felt in his entire lifetime, and Neil was not a man who worried.

"I'm sorry." Her teeth chattered as she apologized

again. This time, tears popped into eyes that were so filled with remorse and loss that he wanted to kick himself for being such a prick.

"Candy, I'm getting really tired of you apologizing every time you turn around. We've got other things to worry about." This time, as he glimpsed her pasty face, he didn't say how concerned he was about infection setting in and the fact that he had no antibiotics, nothing, if she took a turn for the worse.

He shone the light over the ugly-looking wound, which was now red around the edges and looked as if something oozed from it. He pressed around the edge.

"Oh, that hurts!" She grabbed his wrist.

"Candy, it looks infected. I'm going to have to clean it out again." He rummaged in the first aid kit and found some ibuprofen. "Here, swallow these." He dumped three in his hand and put them in her mouth. He grabbed a bottle of water from behind him, unscrewed the top, and held her head up while she swallowed.

Neil slipped a towel under her leg and butt and poured the rest of the water over the puncture, grabbing a towel and wiping away the grit. He poured more water over the wound and squeezed the puncture as he poured until it looked cleaner. Candy groaned and cried out and held his wrist, his arm, but she didn't move, and he was sure it had to hurt like hells fire.

"How are you doing, Candy?"

"Just hurry up. Do what you have to." Her voice cracked, and she sounded tired.

Neil wiped the puncture dry and then squeezed a layer of antibiotic cream over it, covering it with a square bandage. "All done. You did good. I'll check it again in a little while."

Something banged the side of the house with enough force that he felt the floor shake.

"Neil, how bad is it out there? Will the house hold? Is this the worst of it?"

"No, this is a taste of what's coming. The eye of this thing isn't even close yet. We need to worry about the storm surge, and if it stays on course, coming right for us, we have tornadoes and flooding to worry about." He realized then she didn't have a clue about storms, but then, the last one had skirted them while her father was still alive. Maybe he'd taken care of everything. He couldn't remember much, because with Randy around, Candy had been kept at quite a distance from him. He patted her leg. "Sit tight. I need to find us a safe place to hunker down and ride this thing out."

Neil walked out into the large front foyer, looking up at the high ceiling, and shone the light over the orange adobe walls. The house was solid; he, along with his father, had made sure this estate was structurally stable enough to withstand all the hurricanes that ripped through this region. The chandelier with the iron base was a breathtaking piece that hung from the center of the ceiling, but right now, it swayed back and forth, and he had no intention of being anywhere close to it when it came down. It would do some serious damage, cracking rocks or body parts. He walked around the main floor of the house, looking for the best spot to hunker down. It was looking more and more like the laundry room was the safest place, as the stairs were above it. Neil grabbed the duvet and pillows from the guest room, making a bed on the floor against the cupboards in back. He grabbed water bottles from the kitchen and pulled out a bag, filling it with some crackers, granola bars, a bag of nuts, some fruit from the fridge, and he set it on the counter at the back of the laundry room. He pulled out towels and emergency supplies, another flashlight from the cupboard, and left them sitting there. He was ready to move Candy, and he hurried back to where she was lying in the same spot on the sofa.

"Okay. I made us a cozy spot in the laundry room." He scooped her up, blanket and all, while keeping hold of the flashlight. The wind was pulling at the roof—it sounded like metal being ripped away.

"Neil, what about Ambrose? His bottles were in the bag. I dropped them at the door when we came in. He's got to come in here. I'm going to need to feed him. He's going to be so scared."

The donkey, how could he forget? The poor thing was terrified, and he hadn't heard a peep since shoving him into the closet. "I'll get him after I get you settled." Neil set Candy on the duvet, and she lay down, shivering still. "I'll get more blankets, too. We need to warm you up."

Neil went back to the living room and grabbed the first aid kit, the second flashlight, and towels. He pulled out blankets from the hall closet and set them on the floor beside Candy, then tossed a blanket over her before going back for the donkey. When he opened the closet door and found Ambrose curled up, asleep, he realized the animal felt secure in that small space.

Neil carried him back to the laundry room. "Candy, open that cupboard door beside you. Set a towel on the floor there; it's big enough for him to curl up, and I think he'll feel a lot more secure." Neil leaned over her with the donkey and helped lay the plush bath towel on the floor of the cupboard. It had no shelves and had already been emptied of the gear, tents, jugs of water, and sleeping bags, which he'd sent with Carlos and Ana. The donkey crawled right in and curled up.

"Neil, do you have the bottles?"

"Back door, right?"

"I think so. No, I know it is. The bag ripped when I fell, I think." She frowned and seemed confused, and Neil couldn't help but be concerned.

He spotted the bottles—one broken, three rolling on the floor. He scooped up the three and returned to the laundry room, this time shutting the door behind him. He shone the flashlight over Candy, who was struggling to sit up.

She was still shivering, and she reached out her hand. "Give me one of those. I'll feed him now."

Neil set the bottles on the floor and started to hand one to her. "You're not looking too good, Candy. Let me feed him." He moved beside her on the duvet and lifted the bottle toward the donkey, and Candy slid her hand around his. "Never gave a donkey a bottle before. This is a new one for me."

The donkey lifted his head and started sucking on the bottle, and Neil watched Candy, her dark hair a tangled, wet mess. She was clutching a blanket over bare legs, still wearing her rubber boots.

Neil leaned down and pulled them off her feet, setting his hand on her bare leg. "Well, better get comfortable. We're in for a long night."

ELEVEN

Candy was curled up on her side. She could hear Neil rustling behind her, then a clunk as his boots hit the floor. Even though the room was warm, she felt chilled from having been wet for so long. She shivered again, and the cold pulled and pinched in her back, hips, and shoulders, everywhere, every time her body trembled. Another blanket covered her, and she felt Neil's hands brush her shoulders. She couldn't remember ever feeling so taken care of. "Neil, I'm cold. Will you hold me, just to help me warm up?"

He hesitated long enough that Candy realized he was probably trying to find a way to tell her, "No way," that he wasn't interested in her that way. He had to be furious at her for getting him into this mess. She shut her eyes and said, "Never mind. I'm sorry...."

"Stop it, would you?" He moved behind her, sliding his arm under her and pulling her, blanket and all, against him. "I'm just wet, my jeans, and I don't want to make you colder."

"Neil, I'm sorry." She rested her hand on his leg,

touching wet jeans. "You should change. You've been running around looking after me. You could have put on a dry pair, looked after yourself."

"Candy, stop apologizing with every second word." He nuzzled his cheek in her hair, and she could have sworn he was breathing her in, then pressed his cheek against her ear, his breath feathering her hair. "I'm fine. Besides, I considered taking them off, but I figured you wouldn't appreciate it."

She felt her face burn at the thought. It was such a distraction, thinking of him that way, that she almost wished he would.

"Candy?" He must have sensed her distress, and the last thing she wanted him knowing was how attracted she was to him. She wasn't quite ready to admit it even to herself.

"Neil, why did you come for me? You could have been long gone from here, someplace safe."

"I wouldn't leave anyone behind, ever. That's not who I am."

She could feel his warm breath, but she could also feel how tightly he held himself, as if putting a brick wall between them. Something inside her stiffened as she felt a tiny bit of hurt from what he said. Oh, he was saying all the right things, like a knight in shining armor, but he'd do that for anyone. What she realized was that she wanted him to be there, right now, for her. She wanted to be the only reason he had come, to know that he cared. She knew this was just silly, but it was easier telling her mind that simple reason than it was trying to convince her heart.

"Hey, what's wrong?"

She swiped at a tear that had slipped out, hoping he didn't notice, but Neil, being Neil, noticed everything. That much, she'd picked up. "Nothing."

"Oh, I see, we're doing the 'nothing' thing. Gotta tell you, honey, with two sisters-in-law married to my brothers, Brad and Jed, the most stubborn, hardnosed..." He let out a laugh that sounded almost like a groan. "Let's just say that Brad and Jed do some of the stupidest things I've ever seen, and they say things to their wives that get them in all manners of hot water. When I ask them what's wrong, both Diana and Emily say the same thing: 'Nothing.'"

The way he said it had a smile tugging at the corner of her lips.

"Come on, tell me. I know this is usually followed by the silent treatment, which is code for 'What you just said and did was the most insensitive, stupid thing ever.' Candy, I've always been the one who's had to pull my hardnosed brothers aside and point it out when I'm there, mostly out of pity that they'd have a long cold night ahead of them otherwise. So tell me what it is I did, because I'm not insensitive. In fact, I'm caring, thoughtful, a great listener, and pretty damn good looking, as has been pointed out to me a time or two."

Candy rolled over, careful not to bump her thigh, and Neil flicked on the flashlight and set it behind him so it pointed at the ceiling. Candy knew he was right, but being called out on her behavior was hard, especially when dealing with a man as astute as he was. She couldn't believe Neil had picked up on her feelings, and she hoped he couldn't read her thoughts. Even thinking it now had her face heating again.

"Where do your brothers live?" She needed to change the subject fast, distract him from that burning, perceptive gaze that had him watching her so closely that, for a second, she wondered if it was his way of saying, "I want to eat you up, every inch of you."

He raised himself up on his elbow and gazed down on

her. His expression changed to be that lighthearted, fun Neil that she'd never let herself get to know.

"Up in Washington state. Brad is the oldest. He's got the family ranch outside Hoquiam on the peninsula. Jed is outside North Lakewood; he's the younger brother, the stubborn one who set out on his own, scraping together enough money from two-bit jobs to buy a piece of shit dustbowl and run-down house. He set out to prove everyone wrong, saying that he could do it himself, and he did. I admire his guts. I admire everything he's accomplished. Both my brothers, they're the best. Mom and Dad are up at Jed's right now because his wife just had their second baby, another boy. It was rough for Diana for a while because she was overdue. He was a big boy, almost ten pounds."

Ouch was all Candy could think. She watched in amazement as a goofy grin spread over his face. Normal guys didn't get like that when talking of someone's baby. "Do you like kids?" she asked.

"I love them. I have so much fun with my nieces and nephews, two girls and three boys now. Can't wait to meet the newest addition. Didn't hear what they named him. I talked to Mom right before we lost power, and Diana and Jed were having trouble agreeing on a name. I can just see them arguing. But Jed has a way with Diana. He's so protective of her, too, even though she butts heads with him all the time. I know she wouldn't choose any other life."

Candy tried to swallow past the dry lump that had jammed her throat. Just listening to Neil talk about this family, his brothers, she could tell there was so much love there. She couldn't imagine what it would be like to have a husband like that, a family like that. "Wow, it sounds like you have a close family." Even to her own ears, it sounded wistful.

Neil was staring down into her eyes, studying her even though it was dark. She wondered what he saw. Even with the flashlight on, she couldn't see his face clearly, but she could tell he didn't miss how she was feeling.

"Tell me about your family," he said, reaching over and moving a strand of hair from her forehead. His touch was so distracting that she swallowed again, and even though she couldn't see his eyes clearly, she could feel them burning into her, watching her, studying her as if he was reading her every thought. And that scared the hell out of her.

"There's no one." She said it a little too quickly, but the last thing she wanted to talk about with Neil was her father and why they'd left Detroit all those years ago. "Just my horses, and Ambrose here." The donkey sighed, curled up in the cubby beside Candy, as if knowing she was talking about him.

"Why did you stay all by yourself? I mean, it has to be hard for a woman alone, especially out here."

At any other time, she would have probably kicked him or called him all manner of horrible names, but there was something about the way he asked that she believed he had no ulterior motives. "It meant everything to Dad, our place. This is my home. I love it. Where else would I go?"

For the life of her, she couldn't decipher what he was thinking, as he seemed to frown before wiping his hand roughly across his chin. That was all she could tell in the shadow of the light. Every sound in that moment seemed to magnify: the way her heart pounded, even the storm that raged around them outside, whistling, banging, and clawing at the roof.

"Why don't you try and get some sleep? We could be in

for a long night. May as well rest now while we can," he said.

Candy rolled over, and Neil pulled her closer, pressing her back into his chest, the curve of her butt and thighs pressed against him. The chill that had raced through her moments ago eased as she tucked the pillow under her head, his arms surrounding her. She sighed, allowing herself to feel safe for the first time—the first time since, well, she couldn't remember when.

TWELVE

N eil needed to move. Besides the fact that his damp jeans had dried uncomfortably, the agony he felt in the most unbearable of places had him hurting in a bad, bad way, all because the woman who'd filled his dreams for the last few years, and toyed with his every emotion, had her leg tangled with his and had practically draped herself across him, her cheek resting on his chest, her breasts pressing into him, and her hand just inches from the source of his discomfort.

The last thing Neil wanted to happen was for her to discover his problem, one he'd never be able to solve here and now, not without stripping her bare and turning her slim curves over, setting her under him for a distracting and comforting ride. But he couldn't do that, not to her. There was something about her that wasn't just the average pretty face. She was a woman with such deep emotion that she felt everything and took everything on. She could be unreasonable, but she was also the most dependable, supportive, "stand by your man" type of woman, through hell and everything else. She was a woman who could pull every conceivable emotion from Neil, who prided himself on being calm and level headed.

No, Candy wasn't a one-night stand, and she wasn't a distraction, either. He realized that she probably had most guys at a full-out sprint for the hills. She was a commitment, she was a handful, and she was also a very real problem he needed to move, because he was fast losing his sound reasoning to the basic animal instinct of waking her and rolling her over, sampling those luscious pink lips. Except he wouldn't stop there, not with Candy, because he'd wanted her for so long, the one woman he couldn't have.

She mumbled something in her sleep and then slid her hand lower until she bumped the ridge of his erection, and her hand froze. He listened to her breath catch, and in an instant he scooted away and sat up, sending her flying. She cried out sharply, and—idiot!—he could tell she was in pain.

"Candy, are you okay?" He fumbled for the flashlight and shone it on her, and he didn't miss her discomfort.

"My leg is all. I'm sorry, but you moved so fast, dumping me, and I bumped it." Her face was flaming, and he realized she was humiliated. Hell, he was embarrassed. She must think he was some sex-starved teenager, which he wasn't. At his age, he could control that urge somewhat, even though it had been a while since he'd been with anyone.

"I'm so sorry, Candy, but when you moved your hand..." He stopped when she slapped both hands over her face. "I'll be right back." Neil started to stand up because he needed some air, to cool down, to get his head out of his pants and back where it belonged.

But Candy obviously had other ideas, as she grabbed

his arm before he could move away. "Neil, I need to use the bathroom."

Of course she did. They'd both been stuck in this room for how many hours, drinking water, eating the crackers and nuts he'd brought in. Even the donkey must have thought so, too, as his hoofs scraped the inside of the cupboard. "Ambrose, stay in there." She reached in and patted him until he scooted down again.

"Just let me make sure everything in the house is intact. I'll be right back." It hurt to move, and Candy was so inno-cent that he realized she had no clue what she was doing to him.

"Neil, I don't hear the banging I did before. Do you think the storm has passed over?"

Neil opened the door and peeked out, shining the flashlight over the walls and up at the white ceiling. The house was pitch black, as every window was boarded up. He supposed it was the middle of the night. He glanced at his wrist, but the gold watch he always wore was gone. He had no idea where he'd lost it, but then, it could be anywhere, from everything he'd scrambled through yesterday and today. Come to think of it, he couldn't remember putting it on this morning—or was it yesterday morning?—before helping board up the house. Neil walked farther down the hall, listening to the storm outside whipping against the sturdy concrete walls, an awful racket, but everything inside seemed fine. By the time he started back to where Candy was hunkered down, he was feeling somewhat better.

"Okay, there's a bathroom right next to us here. The power's gone, so don't flush. I'll get buckets to dump water down and flush it later. There's water in the tanks, but we can't drain it, because that's all we've got."

Candy struggled to her knees and held the counter as she tried to pull herself up.

What the hell was the matter with him, standing there like an awkward geek, letting her fumble around? "Stop, let me help you," he said. He scooped her up as she dropped the blanket, wearing only his t-shirt and those thin skimpy panties, and she looped her arm around his neck. All her soft warmth and bare skin was doing little to calm him. She breathed sensuality through her innocence, and he suspected there was much more to her, something else she was hiding behind some mysterious wall she'd erected. He'd figured that much out.

He set her down inside the bathroom. "Here, I'll leave you the flashlight." He handed it to her and started to shut the door to give her some privacy.

"Neil, I'd like to wash up. Is there water I could use, a washcloth, soap? I smell like Ambrose."

"Yeah, sure. Just plug the sink. Use a little bit of water from the tap. It'll still work, as there's water in the tank. Don't use much, and leave the water in the sink. We'll have to reuse it for now. I wasn't planning on staying here, so there's no water stocked up, and who knows how long we'll have to count on that water? Once it's gone, it's gone, Candy." Neil opened a cupboard beside the sink and pulled out a washcloth and towel. "Soap is right beside the sink. Stay here until I get back. Don't lock the door. I'm going to check the rest of the house. I won't be long."

He went back into the darkened laundry room and felt around for the second flashlight. He shone it on the big-eyed baby donkey, who started to get up. "No, you stay right there." He patted the donkey and pushed his back end down, sniffing the pungent air around him. Getting stuck in a closet-like room with a donkey and no open windows was, to say the least, an experience he didn't want to repeat. There was a reason donkeys belonged in barns, but Candy's love for animals was a side of her that shone through, along with her passion and her fight-to-the-death attitude. She'd make a great mother. Whoa! He'd better keep that thought to himself. But there was a list of qualities he'd always had and kept in the back of his mind for his future wife. She had to be gorgeous and be the hottest ticket in bed. She had to love children and want to be a mother, his wife, and she had to give up whatever career she had. He wouldn't play second fiddle, and neither would his children. On that much, he agreed with his brothers. She had to be unselfish, and, in his mind, he used his brother Brad's first wife as an example. Crystal was the most self-absorbed schemer, and she'd divided his family for years. No way did he want a woman like that, even if she was the best-looking thing around.

Yes, Candy would be perfect, except...he stopped in the hallway and flashed the light around the foyer at the water dripping and running here and there. How would she fit in with his plans for the resort? He created and put together million-dollar deals, then wined and dined billionaires and state officials. The one thing he knew about Candy was that she wouldn't be caught dead wining and dining and doing any fancy schmoozing for any million-dollar deals, let alone his for the resort he wanted to build on her land. Yup, that definitely could be a problem, just like the stream of water running down the stone wall that led up the open stairwell to the second floor. He shone the light up to the roofline and over the long crack that spread about twenty feet across it. "Shit." This was so not good, and what made it worse was that he was practically blind. He didn't have a clue what was going on outside. He could hear the rain pounding the roof, but it was masked now by the running water hitting the stairs and pooling down. As he walked closer in his bare feet, he realized the floor was wet.

There was another bathroom to his right, off the office. As he walked inside the larger room, he noticed the floor was damp in there, too. He quickly took care of business and used a small amount of water to wash up, all the while frustrated as all hell because there was one thing he absolutely hated, and that was being blindsided. With this storm, he didn't know what was coming their way.

Normally, on any average day, Neil was prepared for anything—like a boy scout should be, his mother had always teased. But Neil liked his world organized. He kept calendars, schedules, lists, and researched everything. He was comfortable when he was prepared, when he was in charge, but right now, with no radio to tell him from what angle the storm was coming in, he was damn uncomfortable. He was strong, capable, smart, able to tackle any problem, but he would snap and growl at anyone when blindsided. This storm that had been unleashed around them, on top of them, was hiding everything while setting its full fury on him. He needed a radio, and though there was a radio in the kitchen, the one he really needed was the satellite battery-operated radio already packed in his vehicle. He had to get it.

He stopped outside the bathroom where Candy was and listened. "Candy, you okay?" He tapped the door.

"Almost done," she said as he listened to water dribbling.

"I'm just going to get a radio...." The door opened before he could finish. She was holding a wash cloth and wearing his cotton shirt, which barely covered the top of her thighs, and that white shirt had never looked better. He hadn't realized how much he liked a woman in his shirt, and for a second he imagined wearing it after it had touched her naked skin. He had to clear his throat, but that image was already cemented in his brain. "Are you done? I want to take a look at that puncture when I get back in."

"What do you mean, 'get back in'? Where are you going?" She sounded scared, and by the way she was squeezing that rag in her raised fist, he could almost sense her panic.

He reached out and slid his hand over her cheek, and she leaned into it. "It's okay. I'll be right back. I'm just going to my SUV. If I can get into it, the satellite radio I need is in the back. I think the wind has died down enough that I should have no trouble."

"Neil, I don't think you should go out."

"Candy, I'll be fine. Just stay here until I get back."

"Be careful." She touched his arm, and he felt the shaking in her hand right before she pulled back, as if she shouldn't have touched him, and glanced away.

He didn't stay, because he could hear the water cascading down the wall, and he worried how deep it would get if it kept running. They'd have to go higher, get above the water, but only if he could find a safer place. If the roof was cracked, would it hold, or was it going to come in on top of them? He didn't like any one of the scenarios running through his mind. This was why people shouldn't stay during a storm. If he hadn't found her, if Stella hadn't called him when she did, Candy wouldn't have survived. She needed someone to take care of her and make sure she didn't walk herself into danger anymore. He nearly stumbled from that thought, because for a minute, he realized that it was something Brad and Jed would say. As he grabbed his slicker from the floor of the laundry room, shoved on his boots, and walked through water puddled at the back door, he realized that he and his brothers weren't so different.

Neil opened the door but leaned into it as he cracked it open. The wind didn't gust like it had, but the rain was falling in buckets. The SUV's front end was pushed against the side of the house. Rain pounded the ground everywhere as he stepped out and pulled the door closed. He shone the light into the pitch blackness, but he couldn't see much through the thick rain, as it seemed to come up from every angle. The back end had a tree branch pushed against the tailgate. He shoved at the branches as the wind-blown rain seemed to have him soaked again. He pulled and yanked on the tailgate, and he tried to shove the thick, long branch jamming against the panel, but it wouldn't budge. He went to the passenger door and opened it, climbing in over the seat, and then shone the light over the supplies, the food, the sleeping bag. Everything he needed to evacuate and hole up somewhere was still there.

He shuffled items and found the box with candles and the radio. There was another first aid kit, and he grabbed the box and the sack of food that Ana had packed. He knew there'd be lots, and he was starving for something more than granola bars and nuts. He paused when he spotted his backpack with a change of clothes. Changing into those would be easier than trying to go upstairs to his room, and he'd been considering it even with the way the water was running down the stairwell. Neil looped the backpack over his shoulder and tucked the sack of food on top of the box, carrying it all back into the house. The door blew out of his hands and smacked into the wall, putting a nice hole in the plaster. He set the box down and leaned against the door to shut it, but the wind didn't carry the same punch it had earlier, and it didn't take all his strength to shut the door. This could mean a few things and was not necessarily good news, especially if the eye of the storm was directly above them.

"Neil?" Candy called out, her flashlight shining at him.

"I told you to stay put," he said rather sharply.

"I was worried, and I heard Ambrose whining. He's scared."

Neil didn't miss the shake in Candy's voice even though she was doing her best to hide it. That was what she did, another thing he recognized about her, another thing he'd have to work on with her. He realized then how much fun it was going to be.

"Look, sorry, just let me put this down and I'll come and help you," he said, but she was already hobbling into the laundry room, and he caught a whiff of her soap-and-water scent. She was an effortless woman who twisted his heart and his sound reasoning around her little finger. And he realized she had no idea.

She held the lip of the cupboard as she sat back down, and Neil set the supplies on the floor and pulled out the radio, not missing her wince as she tried to straighten her leg. "Your leg hurts still, Candy."

It wasn't a question, and she didn't answer him right away. When he looked over at her, she was staring at her hands folded together in front of her. It was too dark to make out her features, but he could see something was wrong: She was worried or upset or something and was holding it all in like she always did. "Candy?" he prodded.

She glanced over at him and forced a smile to her lips, but even a fool could tell she was hiding something, and Neil was no fool. "It's not as bad," she said. "Did you get the radio?"

He didn't miss the way she changed the subject. She was good at changing the focus of attention on her. Most women loved the spotlight, but Candy loathed it. There was a lot he was beginning to discover about Candy that was a window to her soul. He supposed that was why she hid on her property, all by herself. No one should ever be alone.

Neil slid off his wet coat and set the radio on the counter. "You know, you bottle things up so tight inside yourself. I'm here with you. You're not alone, Candy. It's not going to kill you to talk to me, so tell me what's going on in that head of yours."

He tuned the radio, searching for a station but picking up nothing but static. He shone his light on the dial and turned it until he picked up something; he could hear music in the background and left it there, hoping an announcer would come on and give a storm update.

He listened to Candy's breath, her soft sound rustling behind him. He set the flashlight on the counter, shining the light at the ceiling, and turned to Candy, and she was sitting there, staring at her hands.

Neil grabbed the flashlight and moved beside her on the floor. "Let me take a look at your leg. Come on, scoot down." He held his hand out to help her, and when she finally glanced up, there was enough light that he didn't miss the tears she was trying to hide. Whoa, what the hell? "Candy, is it worse? Does it hurt? Let me see." He lifted the hem of the shirt and pulled the bandage away, but it wasn't as puffy and swollen as it had been earlier, although it was red around the edges. He glanced up at her, and she seemed to be fighting to hold herself together. "This looks better. Do you need Tylenol?"

She shook her head. "No, Neil, it actually doesn't hurt as bad. Don't worry about it. It's silly, really. I'm sorry."

If he heard her say "I'm sorry" one more time, he thought he'd scream or yell or something. "Candy, stop with the apologies, already. What is it?" He forced the words through teeth he'd jammed together, because shaking her and yelling at her right now was something

Brad or Jed would likely do, not level-headed Neil who had graduated Harvard with an MBA and could calmly handle just about any situation. But being here with Candy, he was starting to see how much sense his brothers' caveman ideals made, and, in a moment that had him pause, he almost understood them. And that was a scary thought.

He slid his hand around her chin and turned her face up so she was forced to look at him just as a tear slipped out. She couldn't hide it, and he could tell she was embarrassed.

She slid her hand around his wrist, and instead of pushing him away, she held on. "You scared me when you left. I didn't think you'd come back. I thought maybe you'd had enough, too."

What the hell was going through her head? Maybe he hadn't heard her right. Whatever could make her think he'd abandon her after everything he'd done for her so far throughout this storm? "Candy, I'd never leave you. I'm not going anywhere, and I can't help wondering what would ever make you think I could get up and walk away as if it was so easy. You've built up some pretty heavy walls." He watched her as another tear slipped out. "I didn't mean to scare you, but now that I have the radio, I can find out what's going on out there. Being in here now is all fine and great until something catches us unaware. That radio is going to tell me where the hurricane is and which way it's coming so I can figure out what to do next to keep you safe." He watched her for a moment and wondered what was going on in that pretty head that now had her frowning.

"He left me."

She said it so matter-of-factly that Neil had to blink and wonder who she was talking about. He dropped his hand from her chin, taking her hand in his, and sat facing her. "Who left you?"

"Kevin." She shrugged.

Neil couldn't figure out who Kevin was. A boyfriend? He didn't think she was seeing anyone. "Who is Kevin?"

"He wasn't really a boyfriend, but a friend, I thought, anyway. Knew him for years. He was a friend of Dad's. He was always coming out. Did a lot with Dad when he was still running the charter business. We spent time together, he took me out with him all the time in the boat, and, I don't know, I kind of thought maybe one day, the two of us...it was silly on my part. I know that now. When Dad died, I called him, thought he'd come back for me. But now I think it was more about what he could get from Dad. He said he'd take care of me, and he was here when we tossed Dad's ashes in the ocean. I thought I could lean on him, that he cared, and then I found him going through Dad's papers, Dad's stuff. Then he packed up and left, said he was busy, had things to take care of, that it was great seeing me and to take care. He patted my shoulder. He never patted my shoulder. He hugged me, kissed me once, too, and then he walked away as if I meant nothing. I shouldn't have leaned on him. I scared him away."

"He was a coward and a gold digger," Neil said. Maybe this was why Candy was so prickly. Right now, he was furious for her. This prick, Kevin, Neil would have loved to slam his fist in his face, beat the crap out of him. He knew what he was about. Just listening, Neil could tell that the dirt bag only cared about what he could get. Kevin would have hurt Candy badly. He had obviously figured out that Randy had nothing, that he owed people money, that there was nothing of value to be found. But Neil wondered, too, what else that guy had found in those papers, because right now, he was sure Candy didn't have a clue.

"What, why would you say that?" Her eyes widened, and he could see the shock register. "He was a friend of Dad's."

"Do not for one second defend him. No man treats a woman like that, speaks to her like that, and walks away from her because he finds something her dad did that he doesn't like. He didn't care for you. He didn't respect you. He would have hurt you, Candy. Realize that now, and be thankful he's gone. Friends, real friends, stick by you and just listen. Your dad had nothing, Candy, and this guy obviously figured it out. Don't ever settle for any man unless he is madly and deeply in love with you and is all about taking care of you the way you should be taken care of."

She went to say something, and then her breath squeaked. "Oh."

Neil slid the back of his fingers down her cheek and watched. Her eyes dipped to his lips, and he just leaned in and tasted her, his lips on hers. Angling his head, he traced his tongue at the edge of her lip until she opened, and he took all that she offered. He shoved his hands in her glorious hair and held her to him as he sampled and tasted, as her arms slid around his neck. She was really getting into the kiss, her tongue darting out and tasting him. She was driving him wild, and he slid his arm down around her waist, around her sweet cheek, and held her flush against him, her breasts pressing into his chest. Her nipples poked him, and he could feel her need building against him.

Neil slid his hand up and under her shirt, feeling the softness of her skin, and she trembled from his touch and pressed harder, closer to him, as if she couldn't get enough. She moaned, and her fingers dug into his back. He had to tear his mouth away from her. "Holy God, slow down." He felt her flinch. "No, that's not what I meant, but I won't last at this pace. You been with anyone before?" He didn't know why he asked that or why that had popped from his mouth.

She didn't answer, and his hand was still under her shirt, at the side of her breast, circling around and then covering her nipple as he pulled back and just watched her. He slid his other arm around her back, and she nodded.

"I need you to say something, Candy."

She slid her hands on his shoulders and went up on her knees with him, pressing against him and all that was straining in his jeans. He wanted nothing more than to pull off her t-shirt, strip off her underwear, and bury himself deep inside her.

"No, I haven't been with anyone."

It took a minute to register in his brain what she'd just said. He fisted his hand and then slowly lowered it. "Candy, I can't believe I'm going to say this." He slid both hands over her shoulders and then up to cup both her cheeks until she looked at him with such hurt, as if she knew what he was going to say.

"You don't have to say it, Neil. I'm sorry it would be such a chore for you." Her eyes flashed with a fire he recognized, and he could feel her pull away.

"Knock it off," he growled. "I'm done with your apologizing. Stop saying you're sorry as if you and you alone are responsible for everything that's happened, including my erection."

Her eyes snapped wide open as her shock registered, most likely from his blatant description of his body part.

"You are not a chore," he continued, "and if you think about it, you'll realize that I kissed you as I've wanted to for so long. The last thing I'm going to do to you is lay you flat out naked before me and bury myself in you and ride you like an animal, especially since you've never been with anyone. I plan on making love to you, but I want it to mean something, not a quick romp in a darkened room with a stinky donkey beside us. You deserve more. You deserve a proper bed, roses, candles. You deserve to be treasured. For the first time with me, it should be special and be something you remember as magical, wonderful, outstanding. Not this. So just slow down, take a breath, because this won't ever be casual sex, not with me."

"But what if I want you now? What if I don't want everything else?" She licked her pink, luscious lips that were still wet from him.

My God, how could she be so innocent as to not realize what she was doing to him? That simple gesture was the same as waving a red blanket to a bull, and Neil only had so much control. His body had a mind of its own as he dipped his head and ran his tongue over her lips until she opened, and he took and tasted again. He knew he should stop. Somewhere, on some level, his head was telling him to stop, but she was so hot and sexy and slim and luscious, and every curve was pressing tightly against him, rubbing against him. He held her like a drowning man as he slid his tongue down her neck, and she tilted her head to give him more. He slid his hand in her hair and lifted it back, setting his teeth in her earlobe and pulling, and he listened as her breath caught and she gasped again.

Neil lifted his shirt from her and tossed it. He took hold of both her breasts and squeezed, then leaned in and tasted the most perfect nipples, running his tongue over first one, then the other. Her hands were everywhere on him, down his back and then to the button on his jeans, and her fingers fumbled as she started pulling on them.

Static from the radio and the news cut in and out, but

he ignored it for a second until something about it finally registered and cut through his lust. It took another second before he could pull his lips away. He set his forehead against Candy's, breathing as if he'd raced for miles. She slid her hands up his chest, and Neil turned his head to listen. She tried to pull him back.

"No, Candy, stop. The radio, listen for a minute." He moved away and adjusted the dial on the radio until it came in clearer and the announcer's deep baritone gave details of the storm and its shift. The eye of the storm was approaching or was upon them, just north of Cancun. Neil had to keep adjusting as static kept cutting in and out, and he was picking up on bits and pieces.

"Neil, is the storm passing?"

He heard her rustle and glimpsed her pull his shirt over her head. "I don't know. I'm pretty sure, from what I heard, it's moving north. Could be we're just getting the tip. It's still over us. Listen to the rain, the way it's pounding the roof."

"But it's calm in the eye of the storm, Neil."

He turned around and spotted her as she pulled a blanket over her legs, clutching it up to her breasts. He didn't miss her awkwardness. He moved toward her before she could pull any further back into her shell, the one he realized she was racing to now and had cocooned herself in for years, for as long as he'd known her. He lifted her onto his lap. She hesitated only a second before relaxing and leaning into him, waging some war as if she needed to give herself permission.

He realized he was going to have to work on this with her, get her comfortable with him, at ease with herself, before she opened up to him. She'd definitely be a challenge he'd enjoy.

"You're right. It is calm and deceiving, and many fools

have thought the storm was over only for the other side to pass over and be just as bad, if not worse. This is a good thing, because it means we're not getting the worst of it. We're not on the right side, and the storm surge shouldn't be as bad. We're far enough back here in this house that it shouldn't reach us." He was hoping they were. That was one thing he and his dad had made sure of before they bought this place. The resort he planned was a different story.

"Will my place be gone?"

He could feel her looking up at him as if she were waiting for him to tell her everything would be all right. He felt like a traitor, because his development would be easier with her place gone. He held her in his arms, resting his chin on top of her head. She fit so perfectly in his lap, as if she belonged right here and now. "Yes, it will be gone." She stiffened instantly. "Candy, at your place, the storm came right at us. Before we left, I could feel it coming down around us. I'm sorry, there's no way it's still there."

"My horses, what about my horses, Neil? Are they gone, too?"

He hoped they weren't. A house was one thing, but he knew that knowing her horses were hurt would kill some part of her. "I'm sure they're fine. Animals have a sense about this. They would have moved inland, found safety. We'll find them after this is over." That was if they hadn't been trapped by some downed tree, drowned, injured, or killed by flying debris.

"Promise?"

He swallowed, "Yeah, I promise."

THIRTEEN

I t was the slide of his hand down her back, under her shirt, that had her opening her eyes, but not one part of her had the strength to move. Even though she was lying almost naked on top of him, she had no desire to move from the warmth and comfort of his arms.

"I think the storm has passed over us. I don't hear anything," Neil said as his large hand, which was so comforting, slid lower over her butt and over her thighs and back. Then he squeezed gently, and she pressed herself against his leg as he ran his hand up her back and into her hair, pulling her face up to his. He kissed her lips, her cheek, and then breathed in her hair. It was then that Ambrose stepped out of the cupboard and onto her.

"Ambrose, get off!" she yelled at him.

Neil pushed his arm out, bumping Ambrose off Candy, and the donkey jumped over them. The odor that followed as the donkey peed on the floor had Candy burying her face against Neil. Ambrose then bumped the door. He wanted out. Of course he did.

"Okay, that's it." Neil pulled away and sat up, grabbing

the flashlight and flicking it on. He shone it on the radio and clicked it back on, grabbed his boots and shoved his feet in, and then picked up Ambrose and shoved him back into the cupboard.

"We're out of milk for him, Neil," Candy said. She'd given him the last bottle before they went to sleep.

"I'll figure something out. We should be able to get him to graze a bit on some grass or hay. A little bit shouldn't hurt. Just hang tight for a second—I'll be right back." He was standing up now, the flashlight in his hands.

"Where are you going?" she asked, unable to believe he was leaving again.

"Bathroom. Then I'll check and see what's happening outside, if the storm has passed." He was already at the door, and when he opened it, there was a trickle of light.

Just with him mentioning the bathroom, Candy needed to go, as well, after all the water she'd drank and the ham sandwich they'd shared. She wanted to rinse off the grime she felt covering all of her. "Neil, I'm going to the bathroom, too."

He held out his hand and helped her up. The tape pulled around the gauze, pinching her skin, but the ache from the puncture was nowhere near the throbbing it had been last night. She could even put weight on it and walk herself if she needed to, but Neil didn't appear ready to let go of her, and the fact was that she didn't want to stop touching him. She couldn't let go. She loved touching him, feeling him all around her. There was something about him and his touch and his entire way of being that got under her skin. His scent weakened her knees, and when his hand reached out to her, she needed to put her hand in his, to allow his large hand to close around her, feel his strength, and she needed it as much as she needed to breathe. The feeling was so wonderful and powerful that for a moment she couldn't breathe.

She smiled as she stepped with him into the pool of light that streamed in from the back door, the distinct panel filled with golds and pinks. She hadn't noticed it before, but then, yesterday was the first day she'd ever been to this house. In this light, even though he needed to shave, Neil was the sexiest man. He'd had her at hello that morning. He squeezed her hand and then glanced up at the ceiling as he pulled her closer to him as if protecting her from everything. For a moment, her chest tightened and she couldn't speak, because this was how it was supposed to be with the man you loved. She wanted to see where it went with him; she didn't want this to end.

"Candy, come on." He set her in the bathroom and said, "Leave the door open a crack. I'll use the other one. I want to check the house, too. Stay here this time until I get back."

He was gone then, and Candy quickly used the bathroom, ran a little more water into the sink, and washed as best she could: her face, her underarms. She opened the door right up so she could have more light and then pulled back the fresh bandage Neil had put on her wound the night before. She poked around it, but it felt fine. It was a little hard close to the puncture, but it didn't hurt like it had. She wondered if she should take the bandage off, but she decided that with Ambrose beside her, that probably wouldn't be a good idea. She taped it back on and noticed her reflection: tangled hair, dirt smudges here and there.

She ran her hand across Neil's shirt, feeling the soft cotton as it slid over her skin, clung to her breasts, and draped to her thighs. She had seen this same shirt on Neil as it covered his pecs, his six-pack abs, his biceps. She'd felt every hard part of him pressed into her last night, and she wanted him so badly she ached. Just thinking of how much she wanted him had her face flaming. She needed to stop, as she was mortified, thinking of what she wanted him to do to her, to teach her, to show her. If Ambrose hadn't interrupted this morning, she'd have been his.

"Stop it." She rubbed her face and then opened drawers, hoping to find a brush, but there was nothing until she got to the bottom drawer and found toothpaste, toothbrushes, combs, and a couple of hair brushes, too. Jackpot. She pulled out the large, round brush with the thick bristles and pulled it through her hair, which had dried in tangles. She felt as if she were ripping half her hair out, but she managed to have it looking halfway decent by the time she heard Neil's heavy footsteps.

He tapped on her door, and she couldn't help how her stomach fluttered instantly as he took in all of her with a look that said he'd love to spend an hour or even a day, she hoped, getting to know every inch of her. He cleared his throat and then grinned that outrageously handsome smile that lit his face from ear to ear. "The worst is over, by the looks of it. The radio is giving accounts of the damage right now."

"Can we go find the horses at my place? Can we get there now?" She realized it was the first time she was looking to him for help, looking to him to keep her safe, and she struggled for a moment because she wanted it so badly, but at the same time she was afraid it wasn't real. To depend on someone like Neil could be a foolish mistake. She didn't want to go there even though her heart and her head were conflicted. It happened the instant the sun came out, as if their isolation from the storm was gone and everything had changed.

His grin dissolved into something softer and more mysterious. He was so hard to read, and his expression narrowed as if he were studying her and had figured her out. "Whatever's going on in your head, you're over-thinking it. You frowned just now, and you're worried about something. Your thoughts are probably going to some dark places. Don't worry before you need to. Don't do it."

She blinked because she realized he thought she was talking about the horses. She didn't say anything.

"Let me grab some rope for Ambrose. We can't let him wander around loose—way too dangerous right now." His gaze drifted down to her bare toes. "And some clothes for you."

Neil found her a long maxi-skirt one belonging to his mother. It was a beautiful light blue color, a little on the big side, and it went to mid-calf, but it worked for now. She left his t-shirt on and pulled on a pair of his socks and her rubber boots. Her coat was still wet, so Neil gave her his mother's jacket to wear as well.

Neil had Ambrose on a long rope at the back of the house. The rain had stopped, and that was the only reason he agreed for them to go out. Ambrose was grazing the grass, and Candy had been surprised how well he got along with Neil.

"Neil, how are we going to get out of here?"

Trees were down, and branches, leaves, and debris of all manner were scattered and piled everywhere. It was amazing, really, she thought as she glanced around the property, that nothing had come down on the house. The huge swimming pool was emptied, the concrete cracked, and part of a roof, wood, metal, and all kinds of things to be sifted through were piled in it.

Neil's once shiny SUV was scraped, scratched, and dented everywhere. The front end had been pushed against the house. Neil was pulling branches away from the back of the vehicle, clearing a path so they could get out. Candy started pulling at a long branch across the windshield, the glass now cracked, but it wouldn't budge.

Neil came around behind her, sliding his hands over her hips as if he had every right. "Stand back. I'll get it."

He said it in a way that was completely chauvinistic, possessive, and at any other time, she'd have kicked him. But she couldn't. He reached around her and then moved her aside as if she were a china doll. She thought for a second about stomping her foot and yelling at him that she was capable, that she wouldn't break and could help, but she stopped herself because there was something about that simple gesture of being treasured that was so new that she wanted to believe he'd always be there for her. She was almost embarrassed to admit how much she loved it. But she had to remind herself there was a fine line between being looked after and losing who she was. As she watched Neil pull on that limb, his muscles flexing under his light t-shirt as he lifted it off with such ease, she imagined those same arms holding her safely every night, and for a moment she couldn't breathe.

"Okay, that should do it." He opened the passenger door and sniffed. "Oh, man, that's ripe."

Even Candy caught a whiff of the odor left by Ambrose, which had left the fancy SUV smelling more like a barn than the new clean leather smell it'd had before Ambrose relieved himself.

"Let me wipe the seat down," he said.

"Neil, it's okay."

He stepped back toward her and took her hand in his, lifting it to his mouth and pressing his lips to it. "No, it's not okay. You're not sitting on that. What kind of guy do you think I am, that I'd treat you like that?" He went back into the house and returned with a handful of towels, wiping her seat down first and then the floor. Then he dumped the towels in a pile at the back door. "Okay, in you go." He slid his hands around her waist and lifted her in. "We'll see how far we can get back to your place, but there're probably trees down everywhere."

"Neil, what about Ambrose?"

He slid his hands over her cheeks and pressed a hurried kiss to her lips, and she could taste his minty fresh breath. Yummy. She thought she could spend a day kissing him, tasting him, touching him, but then he was gone, calling Ambrose, who was bouncing around on the grass like a puppy wanting to play. Just watching Neil with the gangly, fuzzy baby donkey was the cutest thing, especially when Neil demanded that Ambrose stop playing around and come. The floppy-eared thing absolutely adored Neil, but then, so did Candy. With his strength, his love, this man would be an amazing father. For a second, she saw an image of him with dark-haired children running and tumbling on the grass in the yard, laughing and giggling, and Neil was rolling on the ground with them, tossing them, hugging and playing with them. Her throat hurt, and her nose and eyes misted so she had to blink to get that thought out of her head, because it brought a gigantic ache that tore her apart inside. She wanted it so much, but it was a dream she dared not hope for, not Candy McCrae.

She jumped when Neil appeared in her door with Ambrose in his arms, along with the yellow rope he'd tied around him and the makeshift collar. Candy held out her arms to take him on her lap, and Neil's deep amber gaze stared long and hard at her. She dropped her gaze to her skirt and her hands, too, because the man was so astute that he would read everything about her.

Next, he opened the back door and set Ambrose on a towel in the backseat. "Lie down and stay down," he said, closing the door as if the donkey understood and was going to listen to him. Candy scooted around in her seat and met Neil's gaze in her open door, which took in her and the donkey, letting her know he was very much in charge. That had her swallowing and sitting back in her seat, and then he was leaning in so close, his arms on both sides of her, pinning her there. He was so close he could kiss her if he wanted, and her heart was hammering so hard in her chest that she was positive he could hear it. He said nothing, just ran his gaze down her, and then leaned in and touched his lips to hers softly. It was Candy's arms that slid up and over his shoulders to pull him close, and it was Neil who broke off the kiss.

His tongue tasted her again before he said, "Don't think I didn't notice that totally freaked-out, deer-in-the-headlights look you had going on there, Candy. I'm done with it. I'm not letting you run, slink back away from me, and hide. You're not going there again. Do you under-stand?" He said it in a way that let her know that he'd come for her in that caveman way of dragging her and tossing her over his shoulder, and she couldn't wait for her first time to be with him.

"Neil, I..." She couldn't find the right words to speak without sounding like an idiot, so she gave up and just nodded. With one hand, he held both her cheeks and pressed another kiss to her lips, one that let her know very much that she was his.

Ambrose took that moment to shift on the leather seat behind her and let out a sigh. Neil glanced over her shoulder and, like a good dad, said, "You're just fine there. Lie down." Then he closed her door, and she watched him walk around the front of the SUV, his butt one of the sexiest she'd ever seen, fitted in tight dark jeans, all muscle, with long legs. He had a body that she could stare at all day and craved to touch.

Neil slid under the wheel and glanced back at the donkey, then smiled over at her. "See? He knows who's in charge." He turned the key, and the engine started.

Candy was watching the arrogance, the self-confidence, of the alpha who'd rescued her, cared for her, and was now helping her find her horses. She wondered where she'd ever come up with the idea he was so horrible, that he was a user, a man who'd break her heart after he'd had everything he could take from her and then toss her away as if she were nothing. Her heart ached in that moment as she remembered how much her father, Randy McCrae, had hated Neil Friessen.

FOURTEEN

The aftermath of the storm left downed trees, branches, wood, and pieces of houses, cars, broken plastic, trinkets, and even a garden gnome tossed everywhere along the driveway. Neil didn't recognize any of the broken, twisted carnage, but then, after 150-mile an hour winds whipped through the miles of coastline, picking up everything that wasn't tied down, he was surprised the scene wasn't far worse. The driveway to the main road was long, thankfully, about a half mile, but a storm like this would change that mile to the coast to oceanfront property. Neil had just rounded the corner halfway down when he slammed on his brakes.

"Neil, is that a...?"

"Yeah, a thirty-foot cabin cruiser." He glanced at Candy's wide eyes as her mouth gaped, and Neil's blood filled with what felt like ice water as he stared at the big boat parked between two of the biggest trees on their property. He realized how lucky they'd been, because if the storm hadn't shifted, the chances of that boat being right on top of them would have been pretty damn high. Staring at Candy beside him, he wanted to turn around and hide, keep her safe a while longer as he tried to shake off the cold sweat beading up his spine. The fact that the storm surge had come in this far, they would obviously need to rethink everything, especially when they started doing all the repairs.

He heard Candy's sharp breath, and he glanced over at her again and took in how white her face was.

"Neil, do you think my horses okay? How could anything survive this?"

The destruction was everywhere, piled as if an excavator had dug and shoved everything into piles. Neil had to drive around and over some smaller piles of debris and through some pretty tight spaces, the devastation scraping up the side of the vehicle. "Don't start worrying, Candy. We've talked about this. They're animals, and smart. They could be a long way away, too. This is just stuff. They'll come back home. Animals know how to find their way home," he said, but knew he didn't sound convincing, so he reached over and took her hand in his. The donkey then decided to lean his long head on Neil's arm and sighed. He glanced down at the floppy-eared thing. "See? Ambrose agrees."

Candy leaned down and kissed Ambrose on top of the head. "You do, do you?" she asked him, and he sighed again.

Neil glanced up just in time to slam on the brakes: A tree was down at the end of the driveway, and there was no way he could get around it this time. "Okay, we walk from here." He rested his arm across the steering wheel and looked over at Candy. "I didn't check your leg again. You up to walking?"

She blushed a nice hint of pink on her cheeks and glanced down at her lap shyly. "I can walk. It's fine." She tossed her long hair, and he noticed it was no longer a tangled mess. It fell to her waist in lush heaps and waves, and she smiled at him effortlessly.

"Let me have a look anyway before we go." He was out his door before she could say another word. With him walking toward her, she felt so treasured, cared for. It was a light, fluffy feeling that had her melting in her seat. The clouds still lingered, but the sky was calm after a storm that had filled it with blue and brightness, as if something ugly hadn't just ripped through.

She opened her door and was about to climb out, but Neil grabbed the top of her door and filled the doorway with all of himself.

"Back in." He wrapped his hands around her waist and stepped so close that his legs, his hips, and every part of him were touching her. He smelled so good that she just wished, for a minute, that he would kiss her again. He was sliding his hand up her leg, lifting the skirt up, when she grabbed his wrists with both her hands to stop him.

"Neil, stop. I'm not wearing underwear. I took them off because it was dirty, and if you lift this skirt up..." She was hot and stammering like a schoolgirl, and her face was showing all her discomfort.

He couldn't help smiling at the picture she'd just put in his mind. This wasn't the tough-as-nails Candy he knew who wouldn't hesitate to slap him, slug him, and yell and scream at him. This was a vulnerable, innocent, beautiful young Candy, a desirable, hot woman who was just beginning to show him a glimpse of what she'd hidden. He'd always wondered where she buried that sultry, sexy part of her. This was a daring woman who could be devoted to him, a lover who he'd never tire of, not ever, and she'd been hiding behind a tough exterior, like steel armor meant to scare him away. She was trusting him, he realized, in a way that had him considering the magnitude of what she had opened to him. It was a powerful trust from a woman who didn't trust. She'd been hurt, damaged, and used, and he had a pretty good idea by whom. He touched her cheek with the palm of his hand, and he touched her lips with his and said, "I'm going to take care of you."

Her dark eyes, which shimmered like clear toffee, softened, and she said not a word as he realized she was letting him see her at her most vulnerable. He lifted her skirt and held it just so she wasn't completely exposed. He pulled aside the bandage and noticed the yellow on the white gauze. He ripped it off and sniffed, but nothing smelled off. The puncture had a nice red scab overtop, and the sides weren't puffy or oozing. "Let's give it some air for now. I'll clean it again later. It doesn't look too bad."

He slid her skirt down and lifted her off the seat, sliding his hands down both her arms, and she looked at him in a way that made him feel she'd opened the door to her heart and she was letting him in. She touched his arm, holding on to him as she studied the disaster behind him, and he slid his arm around her waist and pulled her close.

"It's pretty bad, Candy, but let's get going. Don't know what we're going to find." Neil opened the back door and lifted out the donkey, with the rope still around him, then reached over the seat, grabbing a backpack and sliding it on. "Water, snacks, first aid kit. We're not walking ten feet without this right now." If he had a gun, he'd take that, too, but the rifles and ammunition were locked away in a cabinet in the basement, which was most likely under five feet of water. There was a second metal locker in the garage with two other rifles and some shells, but the key was up in his bedroom, and he wasn't about to go back and get it.

He grabbed Candy's hand, linked his fingers with hers,

and started walking. He lifted her over the tree and then picked up the donkey and carried him over. Hand in hand, they picked their way around the debris. Neil guided the floppy-eared donkey, who didn't have a clue how to walk, with a lead rope. It would have been a challenge at the best of times, under ideal circumstances, but having Candy here with him, looking at him as if he were a pure hero, he wouldn't consider for one second leaving her donkey behind. He'd keep her safe along with the damn donkey, a cute, adorable thing who was beginning to look at him the same way Candy did. He squeezed her hand, and she smiled up at him, and for the first time, he saw his future in her eyes.

CHAPTER
FIFTEEN

He was the most amazing man. She was at a loss with Mr. Wonderful holding her hand and caring for her donkey on his other side. Ambrose was, in all fairness, challenged with that rope, but Neil refused to take him off and let him wander. He was right that he'd get hurt. The fact that he cared had her tumbling off that cliff in a freefall she just didn't know how to handle. She held his hand as they walked through what looked like a warzone. Tops were snapped off trees, with branches strewn across their narrow path. Neil picked their way through, helping first her, then Ambrose over and under the trees. The road he'd driven down to her place was now a mishmash of treetops and pieces of wood, and cars, trucks, and boats were sunk in the sand here and there.

"Neil, that's my truck!" She let go of his hand and raced over as fast as her leg would let her to her older-model pickup that was on its side, shoved in the sand as if it were a toy car in a little boy's sandbox. The white paint was chipped and scraped off in places.

"Candy!" Neil shouted, and he had his arm around her waist, lifting her and pulling her against him before she got halfway to the buried truck. "Stop! You're going to get hurt. Look at everything. It's just a truck. Leave it—we need to find the horses. I don't know if we should be heading any closer to your place. Your house won't be there, Candy, so you need to prepare yourself."

She couldn't take her eyes off the truck. It was her only vehicle, her dad's vehicle, and he'd left it for her. Damn him, Neil was right. She stared at the shards of steel and chunks of roof sticking up out of the sand, embedded in trees. She wasn't thinking clearly, but she was pretty sure she'd lost everything.

"Candy, this is just stuff. It can be replaced."

She knew he was trying to reason with her, but he had loads of money and could replace anything he wanted, whereas she couldn't. Couldn't he understand that? She didn't have much, but what she had was hers, and just looking at the debris had something painful stabbing her heart. She'd swear she could feel the warm blood oozing out. It was awful, it was horrible.

Neil slid his arm around her waist as if he sensed her need to bolt, to run and dig through the debris to find what was hers. He was holding her back.

"Come on, Candy." He started pulling her with him, away from her truck, away from the hunks of debris. "Candy, the weather is good now, but I don't want to chance being out in this for very long, not with this guy."

She couldn't answer him, but she did take his hand again and walked for what felt like another half hour until she could hear the waves crashing into the shore. She could smell the saltwater that had revitalized her and been her friend and companion for so many years, and she recognized the opening where the sun, the blue sky, and the water met. Then she froze, as if both her legs were large tree trunks suddenly rooted to the ground, and stared at the devastation. A window, a wall, and a bed frame were piled and buried, standing end on end in heaps. She'd have to sort through it all just to figure out what was what. The ocean had always been such a comfort, a place she spent time every single day staring out into the magic, the power. Now the ocean had shown Candy the true power of what it could do, leaving its ugly mark, taking everything her father had built, everything he'd left for her, and destroying all of it.

"My house is gone." She said it so matter-of-factly, but there was nothing left, just this land, this property. There was no insurance, no security, no assets, just a mountain of debt.

"We'll clear everything out of here. I'll take care of it, Candy," Neil said as he rubbed her arm with his hand, which had comforted her and held her through the storm.

She turned on him, jamming her hands in her hair. "What do you mean, you'll take care of everything? I can't rebuild my house. This was my place. It may not be much to you, but it's all I had. I've got nothing left, I have no money, I can't afford this. You can, with all your millions. This is nothing to you. I can't do this. It's gone now, my place, and it would be so easy for you now to get your hands on this property you've wanted for so long, to build your fancy resort and erase everything of me and mine away as if it were nothing!" she cried. She watched as his jaw stiffened, and she was breathing so hard, every part of her shaking, and it was in those few seconds after screaming out at him, those horrible, god-awful things, where she wished she could take it back. At the same time, she wanted to know what he was really thinking. She prayed in that second that he'd changed and that none of this was about his fancy resort.

As her heart pounded, she waited for him to touch her and tell her it was all a misunderstanding, that he didn't want his resort, that this was about her. She waited for his reassurance, and then his expression hardened. Even Ambrose took a step toward Neil and leaned against his leg, but Candy didn't. In fact, she stepped farther away from him. Her head was still traveling down that out-of-control road of accusations. *Just say it, Neil. Please, just say it,* she willed him. *Please.* But he didn't say a word, and that had her heart taking a nosedive, because now it would be so easy for him to get his resort. He would just have to wait for the foreclosure. She was so far behind, and now with this, and her horses, she felt as if everything that defined who she was had just been ripped away from her.

"Candy, I understand you're upset, but getting mad at me is not going to solve anything. You already knew you were in trouble and so far in arrears on the mortgage that Stella couldn't float you anymore. You were so desperate you even went to Francisco, offering him a piece of this place just to stay afloat. He's got squat, and you were ready to settle for very little instead of coming to me. Then you were trying to sell your horses to take care of some of the back payments. What the hell were you going to do? How were you going to eat, look after yourself? Tell me, because I really want to know. You were done, Candy. You and I both know it. Maybe it's better this way, less painful. It's over, it's gone. You can move on. We'll start a new life, a new beginning."

She couldn't believe the way he spoke to her. His expression was dark, and his light amber eyes sparked as if fireworks had been set off in them. She could even feel the way he held himself rigid, his muscles tightening, but it was what he had said that had her head spinning, and it took her a minute before she understood: He knew things about her that he shouldn't. He expected her to just walk away from this, hand it over to him. Did he not even expect to pay for it?

"You know I'm in arrears. How would you know that unless Stella..."

His expression didn't change, but he did press his lips together as if he were holding on to everything, his secrets. Maybe all the caring he'd shown toward her had been a lie.

"You expect to have this now, don't you? Build your fancy resort, do whatever you want, toss me away. What was this, showing up here, rescuing me, showing me you're this wonderful guy, making me fall for you and then tossing me away as if I'm nothing? It really is a game to you. My father said to watch out for you, that you were only interested in power and getting everything, land, property, putting together your million-dollar deals. He said you'd do anything to get your hands on this place, my place, that you would toss me away as if I were nothing. You killed my father! I can't believe I was so stupid to believe that you came for me because you cared for me. It would have been smarter to just not show up and hope the storm claimed another victim: me. Then you could have just taken everything." Her hands were shaking as she pressed them to her head to sweep back her hair, but nothing would stop the agony that had her head, her face, her eyes, her heart, and everything vital inside her aching. For only one second, she actually considered walking into that ocean and not coming out. She couldn't think, because her reasonable mind was drowned out by the most unbearable hurt, that of having lost his love.

He stepped forward, dropping the rope, and grabbed

both her arms. As he held her, she could feel his urge to shake her. "Don't you ever, ever say something so horrible, as if I'd ever consider walking away and leaving you to die. I didn't leave you here! I came for you as I'd do for anyone. Maybe it's time you hear this: I did not kill your father, and he doesn't deserve to be on that pedestal you've stuck him on. Your father owed people money, bad people, lots of people. He left a trail of debt everywhere. He gambled, he drank. I didn't kill him—your father drank himself to death. You can bet I offered to buy this place. I asked him many times, but what I offered wouldn't have been enough for him. He turned me down because I knew who he was, and so did the people he ripped off. He was greedy. You ever wonder why you left Detroit, why he moved you here? Because he was hiding here. I listened. I knew. Your father wasn't as discreet as he should have been, so he was found, and he knew he was found. He tried to sell you to me."

She slapped him so hard that his face was red with the imprint of her hand. She reacted on instinct because she couldn't believe he would say those things about her father. Randy had taken her and moved here for a better life. He'd protected her from Neil. He'd told her to stay away from Neil, that he'd break her heart into a million pieces, that he was all about money and power and once he had her, he'd throw her away. Her father had looked out for her. Of course he did. So why would Neil make up these vicious lies? "You're a liar! My father loved me."

His expression changed to something distant. She couldn't figure out what he was thinking and why he was saying these things to her. After the way he held her, why would he make up such lies about her father? Why? It was automatic: Her arms crossed in front of her as she stepped back, away from him, and she could feel the doors to her heart shutting.

"Candy, your father wanted a piece of the Friessens. He wanted a share in the resort, in what we were doing, and he was willing to let me have you. He said he would see to it that you came to me willingly, and I could have you as mine. If we refused, he said he'd see to it that I'd never have you. I never knew what he meant, but by the way you looked at me, talked to me, I knew you hated me, and I realized your father had his hand in it. You even said as much. Whatever your father said about me wasn't true. I think you know that deep down, if you're honest with yourself. I've never taken anything from anyone. I don't take advantage of the innocent, and that's exactly what you are, an innocent. I've never in my life taken advantage of someone. I know you know this, Candy, which is why I didn't make any deal with your father. You were inexperienced, and he was using you as if you were some commodity, not his daughter, who he should have treasured and protected." He was getting louder and right in her face.

"Are you telling me you didn't want this place and weren't willing to do everything in your power to get it?" She couldn't believe him, and she was so angry. She wanted to hit him, to throw something at him and make him hurt just like she was.

"Don't start putting words in my mouth, Candy. It sounds like a lot has been put into your head about me. I want you, and I want this resort. We can have it all together, you and me."

She couldn't believe he had said that to her. She backed away from him, tears glossing her eyes, and then stumbled backwards, falling over something that stuck out of the ground. She stared at a broken piece of her shattered china that she loved so much: Friendly Village. It had been her dream, her fantasy, ever since she was a child, to belong to such a fairytale place. She'd spent everything she had over the years to collect every piece in that collection. It was her dream community, where she could belong, with a loving family, children. As she stared at the shattered chunk of her dream, she felt as if she were holding a piece of her heart. There was nothing else to hope for.

"Candy, are you all right?" Neil crouched down beside her, not touching her this time.

She stood up, brushed off the borrowed skirt, and started walking away.

SIXTEEN

Neil couldn't believe what he had said to her, and he couldn't believe he was watching her walk away. This was not how he had pictured things going. He thought they were way past the hating, the arguing, the fighting. Of course she was hurt. Look at the devastation of where her home had been! She'd lost everything. And she didn't trust him.

He spit on the ground, and the donkey stepped away but Neil didn't let go of the rope. He needed to give Candy a minute to cool down, some space to get her head together. Then she'd see he was right. But his head was still spinning from what she'd said. Her father, Randy, had been such a first-class prick. He'd always been shady, and something hadn't been quite right with his charter business. Everyone knew he wasn't just taking out tourists; he was running things, illegal things, and Neil and his dad had always thought he was moving drugs. Stella had said it was guns, while others had said it was anything that would make him money. Candy obviously hadn't a clue, but that weasel had wanted more and more, and when Neil approached him to buy him out, Randy had wanted a partnership, a corner office, and his name attached to the Friessens'. That was something Neil wouldn't have, but Randy said he'd hold out, and with the threats he made to Neil, saying that Candy would never have anything to do with him, well...it turned out that Randy had fulfilled that promise in full, and Neil hated him for it. It was too bad he was already dead, because Neil would have loved to knock him around a bit.

Why couldn't Candy see the truth? He glanced up at the blue sky and then listened to the unsettled ocean as her waves crashed again and again. It was time to move, but when he looked up, Candy was gone. "Candy!" he shouted and then listened, but he couldn't hear a thing. "Come on, Ambrose." He pulled the donkey along with him, skirting piles and headed in the direction he'd seen Candy walk. Why the hell had he taken his eyes off her? "Candy, where are you?" Again there was no answer. "Shit!" he shouted, and he picked up the donkey and started running in the direction she had gone.

CHAPTER
SEVENTEEN

C andy could hear Neil calling her. She staggered as she ran, pushing herself through the pinching and aching from her wound. In that moment, she was thankful for the hurt, for the burning discomfort, because it helped to keep her focused and cleared away her desire to turn around and run back to Neil. Right now, getting as far from Neil as possible was what she needed to do, even though she couldn't stop the tears from flowing freely down her face. Her eyes burned, and she was slapping at the bugs that landed on her, biting her faster than she could move. She didn't know where she was going. All she knew was that she couldn't be near Neil, she couldn't go with him, because the fact was that he'd won.

She wouldn't be able to save this place unless the sky opened up and decided to dump a ton of money on her. She was out of breath when she stumbled and leaned against a palm that was leaning a bit but still standing, and she spotted the rotted-out metal hull of the one boat her father hadn't been able to sell. She remembered the day her dad said the boats were gone, his business was gone, and that it was all because of Neil Friessen, a man with a plan, who was responsible for Randy McCrae losing all his business. All the customers were going elsewhere. He'd been drunk again when he said it, but he'd warned Candy that Neil wanted this place and that not having it was costing him millions a day. Randy had said he was the only one standing in the way of the Friessens having their million-dollar resort, and Neil was determined to get it for nothing.

"He wants you, Candy McCrae, and he'll ask you out, chase you, be persistent, and show you all his charm. But you're smart enough to not be used by the likes of him." She remembered her father telling her this, and it had hurt more than anything to have to listen to what he said. She didn't want to be used by anyone, let alone a man she couldn't help but be attracted to. Then he'd said, "You're nothing but eye candy to him, something to have fun with, a warm body he'll use until he gets what he wants, which is this place, and then he'll toss you away." She remembered all of it so clearly. Her father wouldn't lie to her, so why had Neil said such awful things about him?

Yes, her father drank, he always had, and Candy had always cleaned up after him. Every morning, she had picked up all the empties, stacked them in the shed, cleaned up the puke, his dirty laundry. She had cooked and cleaned for him. She had done everything for her father, and he still left her, choosing booze to solve his problems, problems that Neil had created. He drank himself to death, leaving her this place that she had struggled to hold on to for so long, along with a mountain of debt. None of this made any sense. Why had Neil come for her during the storm, rescuing her and Ambrose and caring for them? She knew Neil still wanted this place, and as she cried and started running again, the reality hit her that the place was now as good as his. He had most likely made a deal with Stella, who she thought was her friend, and he would most likely be able to pick it up for a dime, so she better figure out what she wanted. Money? No, it was never about money. She wanted her place. She wanted to be loved. But she wanted to kick herself, too, for allowing herself to dream of cuddling, hugs, lots of love, family, and something deep and meaningful with Neil. All she'd done was splinter her heart into a million pieces by dropping her guard and letting him in.

She heard an odd scream, and it took her a moment to realize it was a horse. Then she heard it again, and the sound sent a chill racing up her spine. Her legs started trembling, and she had to force her feet to move as she raced down a path that was completely unrecognizable. Then she saw him, Sable, his head poking through branches, what appeared to be dried blood on his shoulder and forehead. She didn't see the other horses, but she didn't miss his wild-eyed look. The whites of his eyes were flashing, and he was snorting. With each step she took toward him, he seemed to become panicked and started yanking on the branches as if he'd been trapped forever.

"Whoa, Sable, easy, boy." She held her hand out and walked slowly, but her entire arm was trembling from the sight of him. She could smell the rotted vegetation, her own sweat, and wondered what he was picking up from her. She'd had her entire world tipped upside down and yanked away from her all in one day. She wasn't the same Candy, and maybe that was what he was sensing. Whatever it was, she didn't know what to do to calm him, and, for the first time, she was terrified of her horse.

"Candy!"

Candy jumped. Her heart squeezed in her chest when

she spotted Neil about ten feet behind her, carrying her donkey. His entire expression was one of absolute fury.

"Don't go near him! What the hell's the matter with you?" He was yelling at her again.

"He's my horse. I'm going to help him. I don't need your help!" she shouted back. She was angry and hurt, and she wanted to hurt him with the same agony that had ripped through every part of her. "I know how to look after my horse. Go away," she said, really trying to mean it, though she ached, too, for his strong arms to hold her, wanting that loving feeling again. She also knew she had to walk away, because this man had hurt her so badly that all of her sound reasoning and common sense had disappeared. She wanted to scream and scream and react, but that wouldn't change the reality.

Neil didn't stop or turn away—he kept coming toward her. "Candy, you can be as mad at me as you want, but you're not going near that horse. You're going to get hurt. Look at his eyes! He doesn't recognize anything as safe. He's completely filled with fear, and you don't know what he's been through. He's traumatized, and you walking over to him is going to get you hurt or killed. Please stop!"

He was almost to her, and she wanted him to touch her, to slide his hands over her bare skin and make her feel things she had only dreamed about but never experienced. She wanted him to tell her she was the most important thing to him. She wanted him to desire her and to come for her, only for her, not because of the land or the storm. Just for her.

She stepped back away from Neil, and his expression hardened and changed into something primitive as he set her donkey down. He kept moving toward her, and she stepped back again.

"Candy, stop. Do not take another step."

But she shook her head, so wrapped up in her waterfall of grief and emotions that she couldn't comprehend what was reasonable. All she could see was a man she loved so deeply, a man she needed to hate, a man who'd taken everything from her. She stepped back again and again, and Neil's entire expression changed to one of panic. He yelled, but the sound was slow motion as she felt herself tumbling backward. Time slowed, and she felt nothing but a rush, consumed by a blur and darkness.

EIGHTEEN

N eil couldn't believe he had just watched and could do nothing to keep Candy from falling. She was just out of reach; two more steps and he would have had her. It tore at his heart, the way she had looked at him with such heartbreak, as if she'd emotionally hit rock bottom.

He'd spotted the shadow behind her and told her to stop, but she wasn't about to listen to him. He didn't know what to say to reason with her. He had been prepared to grab her, and he panicked and yelled when he saw the hole, but she stepped back, her expression dimmed as if she were resigned to her fate. He'd never seen such loss and defeat in someone.

All Neil could do was stand and watch her fall back into the hole. "Candy!" he roared. He dropped the rope holding the donkey and raced to where she had fallen, looking down to where she lay thirty feet below in open water. "Candy, answer me," he shouted again and watched as her head moved side to side, but her eyes were closed, and she was covered from head to toe in mud. Then her hand moved from her head to her leg, and she cried out.

"Candy, I need you to talk to me. Tell me what hurts! Can you move?"

She blinked and looked up at him, and he could tell she was confused. She tried to sit up. "Neil, what happened?" she asked, and she sounded really weak.

"You fell backwards. Candy, are you hurt?"

She didn't say anything for a few seconds, and she set her hands on the muddy wall, her legs in the water. "I think I'm okay." She slid up like an old woman, and he could tell she hurt more than she was saying. She would have bumps and bruises for sure even if she hadn't broken something. She groaned and leaned against the wall, wiping the muddy water from her face.

Neil glanced around and spotted Ambrose a foot away with the rope. "Candy, hang tight for a second, honey, and I'll get you out of there." *Good God*. All he could think about was what this woman had put him through over and over. When he got her out, he was going to put his hands on her and shake her until he put some sense into her. He grabbed the rope on Ambrose and untied him. "Okay, big guy, let's get your mama out of that hole. I expect you to stay here." He knew he was taking a big chance with the donkey. He only offered the horse a passing glance. The animal was hurt, Neil could tell with one look, but he couldn't do anything for him until he got Candy out.

He wrapped the rope around his hand and hoped it would be long enough. "Candy, I need you to look up, honey. I'm sending a rope down. It's coming right to you. I need you to reach up and grab hold."

He lowered the yellow rope and watched the shadowy mud that surrounded her for anything else that was down there with her. The rope dangled just above her head.

Damn it! She'd have to reach up to grab it, as it wasn't quite long enough. "Candy, reach up. It's above your head."

She blinked and moved her head slowly, and then her hand was awkwardly reaching up for the rope. She missed grabbing it a few times before she grabbed hold, and that simple effort seemed to take all her strength.

"Candy, I know you're tired, but I need you to hold on with both hands. Grab hold and don't let go!"

She didn't answer but did as he asked, reaching up and grabbing hold with her other hand. She tried to pull herself up to stand and stumbled. Neil held the rope with both hands, and he knew she didn't have the strength to hold on. For the first time, she looked as if she'd given up.

"Candy, I know you're mad at me right now, but I want you to hold that rope like your life depends on it. Don't let go. I'm going to pull you out of there."

"I hate you, Neil! I never want to see you again." She cried out as she said it, and it hurt him to listen to her heart breaking.

"Candy, you can hate me all you want, baby. I want you to come up here and try to knock my teeth out, to kick me, to fight me. I've never known you to back away from a fight. Come on up here and tell me what a jerk you think I am. Come on!" he yelled at her, trying to make her mad, to get the fire burning in her and her adrenaline pumping so he could get her out of there. He pulled the rope up a bit, and she used it to lift herself up. "Candy, wrap the slack around your wrist as much as you can. Your hands are going to be slippery with all the mud on them."

She listened and wrapped the rope two times around her wrist, but that was all there was. She looked up at him and nodded.

"When I pull, I want you to use your feet on the wall to

push yourself up. Whatever you do, don't let go. I mean it, Candy: Don't let go. Ready?" he yelled.

She took a second and then another before she nodded, and Neil started pulling and pulling. Candy put her foot against the muddy wall, and it slipped, her boot falling off as she dangled.

"Neil, I can't get a grip! The wall's muddy."

"Hang on. I'll pull you up." He pulled as fast as he could, and she held on. Where she got her strength from, he didn't know, but he was so grateful, pulling with everything he had until she was coming closer. Neil dug in and fought to hold her, his arms shaking, he had to dig deep to keep going.

"Neil, I'm slipping! I can't hold on!" Her feet were dangling, her hands slipping on the rope, but she was so close.

Neil let go of the rope and grabbed her with his other hand, but she was so slippery. "Candy, hold on to me. Don't you dare let go!"

She was so close, and he could see her dark eyes and the shadow of fear filling her entire expression, but she was wet and muddy and so damn slippery.

"Neil, I'm slipping!" she cried.

Neil pulled her so hard he thought he was going to yank her shoulder from the socket, and then his arm was around her, under her arms, lifting her out and setting her on the ground. She cried, and he pulled her tightly against him, all muddy and wet and her boots gone.

"You scared the life out of me. Don't you ever do that to me again. Are you hurt?" He held her away and ran his hands over her while she wept.

She started shaking her head and said, "You didn't leave me. You didn't leave me." She burst into tears again.

NINETEEN

Candy had never been so scared in all her life as when she had opened her eyes and gazed up at the halo of light surrounding Neil, as he yelled and yelled at her. Once again, he had been there for her. It had seemed like an eternity that she lay in that sopping, muddy hole, and she felt surreal. It took her a minute to make sense of what had happened to her mind, her body, as she felt lost in a wave of disconnection.

There was fire in his amber eyes, and his expression was a mass of worry. For a minute, she couldn't understand what he was asking and had to wipe the mud the dirty water from her face to see. Her back hurt, her side, her leg when she tried to move, and she felt the energy and will she had to keep going just leave her. Neil was yelling at her again and again, and when the rope had fallen, he willed her to grab hold. And she had done so, slowly using it to pull herself up on shaky legs. She didn't know how he had pulled her up, as she couldn't hold on even when she fought with everything she had left, but he had grabbed her arm, digging his fingers in and pulling her up to him.

All she could do was cry, because he was the first man, ever, to come for her, to care for her, and to not let her go.

She had realized, as she lay in that hole, that she had always been the one to take care of everything. She'd been the parent to her father. She'd looked after him, not the other way around. Even the one guy he had brought around, Kevin, had been so much like her father that he never once protected her, cared for her, or looked after her, not the way Neil had. He was still here, even after all the hurtful, cruel things she'd said. He was holding her as she gripped his shirt and buried her face in his chest.

"What the hell were you doing? I told you to stop, and did you listen to me? Dammit, Candy, you could have been killed. Do you have any idea how I'd feel then?" He was yelling at her again, holding her to him as if he had no intention of letting her go.

"I'm sorry. I'm so confused, Neil. You came for me again even though this is all yours now. I can't do this anymore. I've lost it all."

He pressed his hands against both her cheeks and held them, making her look at him, but her stomach hollowed out as she stared in shock at the tears glossing over his eyes. "I don't give a damn about this place. Don't you get it? It's you I want, always has been. You need to stop this, Candy. I can't keep chasing after you and having you running away from me, thinking I'm a devil who's done horrible things. You don't seem to believe me, so I'm not taking any part of this. I'm walking away from it, but I'm not walking away from you."

Candy wasn't sure what he was talking about. For a second, she felt such loss, until she realized he wanted her. "You want me? Just me?"

"I want you, but not this place. I'm walking away from it, Candy, but I want you walking away with me."

She watched the determination in his face, and then it sunk in: He wanted her. Just her. "What about my place, then?" She couldn't understand, from all the years of him wanting this place, her place, how he could just walk away? It didn't make any sense.

"Let someone else have it, Candy. Don't you think this place has come between us and caused enough grief in your life, in ours? I want to be happy. Don't you?" His face was inches from hers, and she studied him, seeing the passion that oozed from him.

The horse screamed behind Neil and started yanking, trying to break free of the tangled branches he was stuck in.

"Neil, my horse, he's hurt."

Neil slid her off his lap. "Stay here. Don't get up. I'll get your horse." He grabbed Ambrose, who was jumping around, and tied the rope back around him. "Can you hold him?"

"Of course." Her arms ached, every part of her. She held the rope and pulled the donkey in her arms. "Come here, Ambrose."

She was shaking as she set her hand on the coarse gray fur of the little donkey, and she watched Neil hold his hand out and walk slowly and confidently toward her horse, talking in a reassuring tone she hadn't heard before. The fact was that she didn't know whether Neil knew anything about horses, and she watched him approach her Azteca as if he'd worked with horses all his life. He got hold of Sables' halter and pulled off several branches pinning him in. He jumped and tried to break free, but Neil held him and talked to him, comforting him, and then petted his forehead, talking softly in the same voice he'd used with her. Sable lowered his head and stopped fighting him, standing there, but she could see how freaked out the horse was. He was trembling, and she could also see that he might go off like a rocket if the wind, a branch, or anything touched him the wrong way.

"Candy, I need you to promise me you'll keep Ambrose really still, and I don't want you moving at all. Can you promise me that right now?" He was talking so calmly to her as he kept his attention on the horse, holding the halter so tightly that the horse stopped fighting him.

"I promise I won't move. Be careful, Neil. Is he hurt?" she asked.

"He's got a lot of cuts all over him, but when I move this branch, he'll be able to get out. I have no lead rope, so he's going to take off. I want you to get up slowly, Candy, and stand over by the tree behind you, and keep Ambrose there. Can you do that?"

She'd crawl if she had to, and her legs trembled as she scrambled in the sopping wet skirt stuck to her legs, the mud clinging to her. She barely had the strength to stand, but she did it, her body aching in spots it hadn't before.

"Candy, you okay?" he asked very calmly.

"Yeah, I'm okay. We're at the tree."

Neil moved the last branch, and the horse jumped out. Neil didn't try to hold him as the horse, her horse, raced away into the trees and out of sight. Neil jogged over to her and slid his arm around her waist, lifting her in his arms. "I'm taking you home now, Candy."

"Neil, what about my horses?" She looped her arms around his neck and held on to him.

"I'm worried about you, and the horse will be fine for now. He's out. I'll come back and get him and look for the others, but you're not coming back here." He tossed her a bit in his arms to get a better grip on her, holding her a little more tightly to him as he gripped the rope tied to Ambrose.

"Neil, I can walk. I'm too heavy for you."

"No, you're not walking, and you're not fine." He pulled her closer, and she loved the feel of his strong arms, at the same time feeling ashamed of how she had acted.

"Neil, I'm sorry." She rested her head on his shoulder and didn't miss the way his jaw hardened and how rigidly he held himself.

"I told you to stop apologizing. For the first time ever, you have me wanting to shake you, and never before in my life has a woman scared the life out of me the way you have."

She snuggled closer into him, all sopping and muddy. She could feel it in every crack and crevice of her, and she shivered. He pressed a kiss into her muddy hair, and she, for the first time ever, just let him care for her.

CHAPTER
TWENTY

Neil pulled off all the shutters from the windows and tossed them on the ground to allow some light into the house. They had a generator in the shed in back, which he fired up after they got back with enough gasoline, he figured, to run it for the next week, if he didn't get carried away. And that was the million-dollar question: How long would it be until power was restored to the area? Weeks, maybe.

He'd carried Candy most of the way back, alternating from carrying her in his arms to having her ride piggyback. Even then, she rested her head against him. He was worried her fall had hurt her more than she was saying. It had taken him almost an hour to reach the SUV, and by the time they got back to the house, he was exhausted and she was a mess, from the crying she'd done to the mud drying on every part of her. She was weak and shaking.

There was water on the floor in the grand entry, puddles here and there at the foot of the stairs. With the rain gone, there was no more water coming in, thankfully.

Candy was weaving beside him, holding his hand. He yanked one of the Queen Anne chairs over. "Here, sit down. I need to check some things in the house, and then I'll get you in a bath and fix you something to eat." He touched her cheek, which was covered with every manner of dried mud and dirt, and she leaned into his hand with remorse and sadness. "Hey, it's going to be okay."

She met his gaze, and her eyes started watering again. "Neil, I'm so sorry I said those horrible things...."

What hurt the most was how confused she looked, but he knew he was getting through to her. It didn't help that he still wanted to kick her father's ass for playing with her head the way he had. He didn't ever want anyone to hurt her again.

Ambrose started chewing on one of the large potted plants against the wall. "Whoa, don't you start eating that." He picked him up and moved him back into the closet, pulling out all the shoes stuffed in the bottom. He shut the door and then went for a bowl of water and a towel, setting it in there with the donkey.

"Neil, is Ambrose going to be okay in there?" She hadn't moved. She was actually, for the first time, listening to him.

"He'll be far more comfortable and secure in there."

She nodded and then appeared to be thinking. "Neil, there's no more goats' milk for him. What are we going to do?"

He took her hands in his as he knelt down in front of her. "Candy, he's going to be fine. He's got fresh water. I'll feed him some carrots later and then get him out to graze again. He will be okay." He tried to reassure her, but the fact was that he was far more worried about her than he was about Ambrose. Unlike her, the donkey was doing fine.

"Come on." He lifted her, and she went easily, linking her arms around his neck, leaning her head against his shoulder.

"Where are you taking me?" she asked as she gazed up at him.

"To my room, where I'm going to bathe you and put you to bed."

He carried her up the stairs and was surprised how intact the hallway leading to his room appeared to be: the woodwork, the tiled floor, the artwork up and down the hallway. They walked past the five doors leading to the guestrooms and his parents' room and headed toward Neil's room, a set of suites at the west side of the house, overlooking the pool and gardens in back. His room was dark, as shutters still covered the second-floor windows. Neil flicked on the light and didn't miss Candy's sharp breath.

It was a nice room, with a four-poster bed, a fireplace with two leather chairs in front, a dark oak armoire, a chest of drawers, and a heavy green carpet in the middle of the room. It was tasteful and comfortable, and Candy was shaking again. "This is your bedroom? It's nice."

By the way she said it, he could tell she was having trouble with his material side. Other women would love it, but not Candy.

"You should see the bathroom." He flicked on the light in his en suite, and she gasped. It was huge, with a square jetted tub, the shower glassed in with steam and five showerheads. In the center of the bathroom sat the vanity, with a glass top over pebbles and a sink in the center. His walk-in closet opened on the other side, with shelves filled with all manner of expensive suits and casual clothes. But then, Neil liked the finer things. By the look in Candy's wide eyes, which resembled those of a startled deer, he supposed she might be having trouble with all that. Not only did Neil want her there and have every intention of keeping her there from that day forward, he realized the real work would be in getting her comfortable with all of this.

TWENTY-ONE

C andy was holding on to Neil, taking in all the glamor, glitz, and wealth in this one room alone. His bedroom and bathroom were larger than her entire house. The detail, with every furnishing right down to the toothbrush holder, cost more than she'd ever see in this lifetime. Even the man's clothes—she'd never seen anything like them. He always dressed well, sharp, expensive, but with the amount of clothes he had, he'd never have to wear the same thing twice. Then there was her tiny, rickety dresser that had held her entire wardrobe, which consisted of two pairs of jeans, a skirt, four t-shirts, a couple blouses, and two pairs of shorts. For her, this had meant less laundry. It was easy. But this side of Neil, this extravagance, she didn't know if she could handle it.

He set her beside the tub and then glanced at the shower. "I think a shower would be better." He opened the large glass door and turned dials and knobs, and water and steam poured out of all the showerheads. It was glassed in, and the ceiling was fitted with a large sunroof. The shower itself could have fit an entire family. What in the world did someone do with a shower that large, walk around in it? She knew she was staring—gaping. Her body, her head, her sharp mind were all fried from the emotional roller coaster she'd had and from the fall down that big hole Neil had pulled her out of.

Neil lifted her stiff hair. "You okay? Because you've got that over-thinking look happening again. What's up, Candy?"

How did she tell him she was having trouble with all his stuff, all this elegance? She was afraid of touching and breaking something. She looked around the room again and then over to the shower, swallowing the dry lump that felt like sand and grit jammed in the middle of her throat. "Ah, you know..." She didn't know how to put it into words, and he tilted his head, giving her one of his looks that made her feel as if he were reading her very thoughts.

He kicked off his boots, pulled off his shirt, and then scooped her up and carried her into that spacious shower, setting her under the showerhead with him. She couldn't help but stare at his chest, with light brown hair over his sculpted solid muscles trailing down to six-pack abs. My God, just looking at that bare skin was better than she had imagined. She pressed her hands flat against his chest and gazed up at him shyly as he seemed to hold himself back, watching but letting her touch him. He ran his hands in her hair, lifting it and rinsing out the mud and grit. Then he lifted her shirt over her head and slid the skirt down, tossing both in a heap in the corner of the shower. She was naked before him, and she started to cover her breasts, but he took hold of both her hands and shook his head.

"Don't. You're beautiful, every part of you." He picked up a bar of soap and washed her down, taking care around her puncture and checking every part of her for scrapes and cuts. "You got a lot of bruises from your fall. Anything hurt?" He skimmed his large hands down her side and back up as she rinsed off the soap. "No, I just feel a little stiff, but this shower helps. Is there enough water to be doing this?"

"Hmm, for now. With the generator running, we're pumping water from the well. I'll check it after we're done." He shampooed her hair, taking such care of her that the lump in her throat started aching and she wondered if she'd start crying again.

"Why are you looking after me? I don't know how to handle this, Neil." She glanced up, and his expression had changed into something predatory and protective and consuming. He lowered his lips to hers, pressing hard and flicking his tongue as she opened for him in a deep, possessive kiss that left her breathless. He pulled his head away and rested it against her forehead.

"You still have no idea. I want you every day. You've never had anyone to look after you. I knew it, I suspected it, and it's not right. You should be treasured." He slid his hand over her breast and lowered his head, taking her nipple in his mouth, and she thought she'd explode from the need burning in her center. The water ran over her, over him, and she gasped, pressing herself closer to him, into him. Her senses were jarred by the jeans he still wore.

"Neil, take off your jeans. Please." She reached for the button, and he brushed her hand away and stepped back from her, undoing the button and taking off his pants. Her mouth gaped at the size of him. She stared and wondered, as she glanced back up at him, how it was possible he'd fit.

He must have sensed her shock, because he grabbed the soap and washed himself, then took her hand in his and set it on his chest, running it over his stomach, guiding her to feel him. In those seconds that felt like an eternity, his eyes never left hers. He took her in his arms and back under the spray of two showerheads, rinsing them off. Then he flicked off the shower. Grabbing a thick towel, he dried her off, wrapped a towel around his waist, and then he carried her to his bed, laying her across the center of the deep green duvet. He laid her down so softly, caringly, and gently. Then he was hovering over her, his arms above her, looking down on her, something so deep burning in those amber eyes that her heart squeezed and cracked open just a bit. She needed to reach out to him and let him in.

She touched his face, his cheek, which was heavily whiskered and scratched against her palms. He turned his head into her hand and pressed a kiss with his lush lips, which knew how to kiss her, and she wanted them on her.

"Please make love to me," she said, watching and waiting while he stared at her as if deciding. She sucked in her bottom lip between her teeth and worried it.

"Candy, I want you so bad, but there won't be anything casual here. If I make love to you, you're mine. Do you understand? There won't be any running away. I won't let you go. I will be demanding and possessive and…"

"Yes." She cut him off before he could finish, sliding both her hands in his wet hair and pulling him down to her.

He took her in a kiss that showed her he meant what he said, deep and consuming, sharing his breath and letting him have all of her. He ran his hands down her side and pulled her to him as they lay side by side on the bed. He lifted her leg over his hip as he kissed her, holding her to him, his tongue touching, tasting her. He kissed her neck, tracing a path down and around her breasts, cupping them in both hands as he took his time pulling on each nipple with his teeth and then running his tongue over them.

"Oh, Neil, that feels so good." She wanted him so badly that she could feel something coil and wrap tightly, deep inside her belly. It was burning and spreading out in a way that made her feel as if she were losing control. She thought she might have bounced off the bed if Neil hadn't rolled on top of her, pinning her under him. He still had the towel wrapped around his waist, and she wanted it gone as she moved her legs apart for him.

His hands were there, spreading her, touching her, feeling her. He was watching her in the pool of light that drifted from the bathroom. She needed his mouth on her again, and she tried to pull him back to her, almost frantic with need. She slid her hands to the towel and tried to pull it off, but he grabbed both her hands and pinned them above her head with one hand while he pulled open the towel and tossed it to the floor.

Again, she glimpsed the size of him and felt him resting against her thigh, thick and heavy. "Neil, I know the mechanics of how it works, but..."

"Shh." He stopped her, and he obviously understood her worry. "Just enjoy. Trust me, okay?"

My God, how could she not trust him? He still held her hands above her, and he lowered his head to her breast and tasted her. He spread her legs wider, his hand there, pressing into her. She felt his finger test her, and she nearly exploded under him, lifting her hips.

"Please, Neil. I need you."

He let go of her hands and pressed her legs wide with both hands, holding her down and settling between her thighs. He kissed her again, a deep kiss, as he entered her slowly, a little at a time, with small thrusts. He froze above her, pressed his forehead to hers, breathing hard, deep, and then, with a sharp thrust, he was in her, and the pain was instant. She cried out, and he watched her.

"Shh, baby, just lie still. It'll pass." He kissed her cheek, her eyes, her lips, and waited until she stopped fighting him.

He was so big and filled her so completely that it was almost too much, but she needed more, something more, and he must have known. He started to move slowly inside her, watching her with such caring and with something else that was a lifeline linking them together. When she tried to wrap her legs around his waist, something that felt so instinctive, he pulled them away and set her legs wide open for him, and he moved inside of her faster. She could tell he was holding himself back, trying not to hurt her, and it felt so damn good, but she was pinned and completely at his mercy. She felt fireworks building inside of her, and he was the only man, the only one, who could release them. She cried out again as wave after wave convulsed through her, and he grunted above, yelling her name, and she felt such warmth fill her. He collapsed on top of her, pressing all his weight into her, still inside her, and for the first time in her life, she truly understood what it meant to be possessed entirely by the man she loved.

TWENTY-TWO

Neil thought for a minute that he'd gone blind. He'd never in his life had his heart connect with a woman while deep inside of her. He could almost feel the way she opened to him, as if she had no control over the heavy wooden door that had been the gatekeeper to her heart. It was so powerful that it was beyond words. A magic that felt like a million firecrackers lighting up every part of him. Even though he had been her first, there was something so magical about the fact that no other man had touched her so intimately. He had been the first to lay claim to her, and she was his. He could understand that Neanderthal, caveman way of thinking that often appeared among his brothers. If any other man ever tried to touch her, he knew without a doubt that he'd kill him. She was special, she was his, and she was the first woman he'd ever brought into his bedroom in this house, the first to ever grace his bed.

Oh, he'd slept with plenty of women. But there was one thing about sleeping with them and having some fun and another thing about bringing a woman home to his bed. To him, having a woman in his bed, under his roof, was a commitment he hadn't been ready for until he met Candy. There was something about her that spoke of family, of forever. He rolled over, taking her with him, pulling out of her. She hissed, and he worried for a second that he'd hurt her.

"You okay?" he asked her and pressed a kiss to her forehead, running his hand down her wet hair, which curled at her waist, and over her slim, rounded bottom. He loved her ass, just touching it, feeling it. She lay on him as if he were her bed, resting her palm on his chest. "Candy, did I hurt you?"

She turned her face up and gazed at him, and what he saw in her eyes had him swallowing his heart. "I feel wonderful, like I belong to you. I'm sorry this was so new for me. Was it okay for you?"

She was worried about him. He wanted to laugh and roll her over and make love to her again, but he had to remind himself she'd be sore. She wouldn't be walking if he was riding her over and over. "Oh, don't you worry about me. That was wonderful. Do you have any idea how special it is that I was your first? That's a gift."

However, he'd also used no protection, and she had to know it. He knew it—he had planned it that way, which was rather selfish on his part, but he was determined to have her, to tie her to him. He slid his hand over her belly, and she pressed her hand over his.

"You'll make a wonderful father, Neil. What if you got me pregnant?"

Yeah, she knew, all right. "I hope I got you pregnant. I hope my child is growing now right here. I already told you I won't let you go now."

She slid up, her breasts pressing into his chest, and she kissed him, then smiled as she looked down on him. "I hope you did, too. I want your child." She looked at him with trust burning in her eyes, which were filled with color and light and passion.

He rolled her over. "Well, let's just make sure we did it right."

CHAPTER
TWENTY-THREE

Candy was sound asleep, draped over him, her leg tangled with his, her hand resting on his chest. He slid his hand over hers, his arm around her, holding her close to him. He'd pulled the covers up over her and listened for a few minutes as she settled into a deep sleep. For the first time, he felt connected to someone he knew he could spend the rest of his life with.

He'd wanted nothing more than to settle in and hold her, to shut his eyes and then wake her up, taking time to explore and taste every sweet inch of her, but he couldn't, because he promised Candy he'd find her horses. He'd already cooked a steak for them to share, along with a salad, after he fed Ambrose. He turned the generator off after cooking, and they ate in his room, off one plate, surrounded by a sea of candles. He fed her, cutting a piece of meat and then salad, putting it in her mouth as she sat naked with the sheet draped around her waist and her long hair draped over her breasts. It was so alluring and sexy, that he'd wanted nothing more, when they finished, than to roll her on her back, spread her legs, and take her again, but he knew she was sore from the two times he'd filled her already.

He held her until she drifted off, but he couldn't wait any longer. He knew that gray horse, her prized Azteca, wasn't doing well. He had cuts all over him. He was freaked right out, and Neil could only imagine what he'd survived out there, racing from downed trees and getting pinned like he was. Horses who were left and stuck alone had been known to go mad, and it took years before they recovered enough for people to ride them.

Neil held Candy and eased her onto his pillow as he slipped out of bed. He sat on the edge and pulled on a pair of jeans, and she slid her hand up his back.

"Where are you going?" She sounded groggy, tired.

"I'm going to find the horses. You stay here. I'll be back." He pulled on a t-shirt and a pair of socks, and Candy sat up.

"I want to come with you." She slid her legs over the side of the bed.

"No. I need to move fast, Candy, and I can't be worrying about you. I need to know you're safe back here." What he couldn't tell her was that he planned on taking the rifle he kept in the garage with extra shells, because he might be forced to put any one of the horses down. Who could know if the others were still alive, if they were lying injured and trapped somewhere he wouldn't be able to rescue them? "Slide back under. You've been through hell today, and I know you're sore. So, back in bed. Get some rest."

She hesitated and then linked her fingers with his as she slid back in bed, resting her head on his pillow. Neil tucked her hair behind her ear before leaning down and kissing her, lingering until she slid her arms around his neck to pull him closer. He reached up and unhooked her arms, kissing each of her hands.

"You sexy siren. Stay put. Do you understand? I don't want you traipsing around outside. Will you promise you'll get some sleep?"

"Okay. Neil?" She smiled and looked so trusting as she lay in his bed.

"Yeah?" He stood over her and held her fingers with his.

"How do you know so much about horses? I mean, I watched you with Sable, and I have to tell you it was the first time I was ever so scared. I've never seen him like that, but you just walked in talking to him like he understood you, as if you were going to make everything okay, and you got him out. I couldn't have done that. He was scared of me."

Neil sat on the bed, resting his hand beside her hip, cradling her against his body. She had a sparkle in her eyes as she watched him, waiting for him to tell her some secret, a woman who had handed him her heart. "I grew up with horses. Trained them, me and my brothers. We're ranchers by blood. Sable was terrified, Candy. Whatever he saw scared the hell out of him. He was depending on me to get him out, but he was so freaked out at the same time. I understood that, and he needed to know I was calm and that I was going to get him out. There is a lot to horses, how they react to you. They read everything about you. Candy, you were a mess when you found him. He would have picked up on that, but you already know that. I better go. I'll be gone for a few hours." This time, he pulled away and started to leave.

"Neil?" she called again as the sheet rustled.

He wanted to laugh. "What now?"

"No one has ever taken care of me before. I just thought you should know."

"Well, get used to it." Neil took a set of keys from his top drawer and pulled open the door and watched her in the dim light, taking in her sexy smile as she wrapped her arms around her knees and watched him leave.

Neil didn't drive to Candy's this time. He had an idea where to start looking for the horses, but he needed to do it on foot. He stopped first in the garage and unlocked the cabinet taking out the rifle and filled a backpack with extra shells, a water bottle for him, and the first aid kit. He slid open the second storage locker that held his old riding gear, his first saddle, which he'd never part with, and old, worn tack from his first horse. His father understood why he had brought it with him and his mother hadn't said a word. He could have left it all at Brad's, the home where he grew up, but it just didn't feel right. He knew one day he'd have horses again; it was just that in the past few years, his energy had been focused elsewhere, like toward the ten-million-dollar resort he had planned to build where Candy's home had once been.

He grabbed a couple lead ropes and a halter, too, just in case. He stuffed those at the top of the backpack and sprayed a heavy coat of mosquito repellant over every inch of him, pulling on a light jacket before he looped the rifle over his shoulder. Neil glanced back at the house before cutting onto the path that would lead him back to Candy's. The horses could be anywhere, but one thing he knew about horses was that they knew how to find their way home, and Neil was counting on that. He picked his way over downed trees and piles of debris that had him zigzagging back and forth. He kept his eye on the sun, watching as it dipped lower on the horizon, because the last thing he wanted was to get stuck out there when the sun went down. There were too many unsettled things after a storm, animals, snakes, nothing he wanted to toy with in the dark.

He spotted what he thought was the wall of the old barn. As he stepped closer, he shook his head at the crumbled debris piled here and there and the chunks of rock that appeared to be holding up the one wall left standing. He was glad Candy wasn't with him, because her horses never would have survived in there. They'd have been crushed, and that image was something he didn't want in Candy's head. No, he'd make sure this was cleaned up for her. It was just one more thing he needed to look after. The fact that he'd promised to walk away from this property and from everything he'd planned and worked toward over the past two years.

He heard something through the trees off to his right. A branch moved, and he saw leaves swaying. He slid the rifle off his shoulder and checked to make sure it was loaded, then stepped over the vegetation scattered everywhere, his footsteps crunching and cracking the leaves and branches scattered all over the ground. There he was, watching Neil. His sleek gray mane was gnarled and muddy. He yanked off leaves from a bush and was munching away. Neil stepped closer and looped the rifle back over his shoulder. He unzipped the backpack and pulled out the lead rope.

He could tell the horse was nervous, and he could feel that Sable was considering bolting. He had dried blood here and there on his forehead, shoulder, down his leg and his flank. The poor guy. Neil was worried about how badly he was hurt. "Whoa, easy, boy. Sable, I'm not going to hurt you." He held his hand out and walked slowly.

Sable snorted and stomped his front hoof, pawing at the ground. Neil didn't stop. Sable appeared wild: The whites of his eyes flared, and he tossed his head. Neil held his hand to his muzzle, then ran his hand up his forehead and over the white star between his eyes, clipping the lead rope to his halter. "It's okay, boy. I'm going to take you back with me."

Something shiny flashed off to the side. Neil held the lead rope and ran his hand down Sables' flank when he spotted the hoof a few yards away, sticking out from under a mangled heap of trees, branches, and part of a roof. "Shit."

He led Sable to one of the palm trees still standing and tied him to it securely. He patted his side and quickly surveyed the cuts and dried blood. He was a mess, but it looked superficial. He should be okay.

Neil made his way closer and spotted the dark leg of one of the horses. It wasn't moving, and as he lifted a piece of rubble, he saw the horse was buried underneath it. He knew it was already dead, the thoroughbred she'd been trying to sell. He didn't know how he was going to tell Candy. She was going to be devastated. Well, there was nothing he could do for this guy. That left the palomino. Neil picked his way around another tree and looked around at the broken-off tree limbs, smelling rotted vegetation and the salty air from the ocean. There was an odor of death, of destruction and decay, that he couldn't shake. He glanced back at Sable and knew he sensed the same thing. Neil didn't want to keep him out here much longer.

He stopped and listened, looking around in each of the four directions. He heard something as he stepped out of the trees to a pile of sand and the palomino who was on the ground, her eyes blinking, lying on her side. He could tell by the angle of her back leg that it was broken. She was barely moving. She had a tree branch poking from her side and a piece of metal jutting out of her windpipe. She was wheezing, barely alive, as he kneeled down beside her.

"I'm so sorry there, girl." He ran his hand over her mane and down to her whither, and she nickered softly. His throat squeezed and threatened to choke him. He blinked back a burning in his eyes and fought the tears that wanted to fall. He stood up, slid the rifle over his shoulder, took off the safety, and pressed the barrel to her head. He pulled the trigger, and the blast left him numb as he stared at the now still horse and the lifelessness that came over it instantly. He hoped she was at peace, and he shut his eyes for a second to steady himself and then headed back for Sable. His heart had been ripped wide open in doing what he had to do.

TWENTY-FOUR

"There are some things she just doesn't need to know." Neil stood side by side with Stella, who, for the first time, wore slacks along with those wretched high heels. He had no clue how she strutted around at her age, and he watched as Candy walked Sable on a lead rope around the corral Neil had put together with Carlos, who had returned with Ana the morning after the storm.

"So you're not going to tell her the truth," Stella said as she crossed her arms, wearing a bright green sweater.

"She doesn't need to know what happened to her horses. It's best if she believes they've found a new home. She lost too much. She's carried an awful lot of hurt for a long time, and I'm not adding to that." Neil glanced down at this colorful older woman he thought of as a friend.

"Is that what you told her?" she asked.

"I said they were rescued and they were in a good place."

"She'll be furious when she finds out."

"I can live with that. What I can't live with is seeing the

pain of loss in her eyes. I don't ever want to see that there again. So, tell me, with the roads now cleared from Cancun, has most of the power been restored?"

"Changing the subject, Neil, will not work with me. You know that." Stella gave as good as she got, and she stood right beside him. The top of her head, even in those ridiculous heels, barely reached his shoulders. "I'm glad to see she's with you and you're looking after her. I knew you two belonged together." She laughed a husky laugh. "Can't wait to see some dark-headed little Friessens running around."

Neil set his hands on his hips and grinned, because he'd spent every night for the last week making love to her passionately, fiercely, teaching her all about love. Not once had he considered using anything to protect her, because the fact was that he couldn't wait to see her belly swell with his child. He couldn't wait to fill this house with his children. He was thinking five, and he knew she'd be a damn good mother.

"I have never seen you this way, Neil Friessen. She's got you, and you have that look about you that says you're going to have her for dinner." She patted his arm. "Thank you. But we need to talk about her property and Randy."

Neil had known this was coming. He took his eyes off Candy for a few seconds and didn't miss the hard set of Stella's face. At times, she could be all business, even though, deep down, she had a heart of gold. She was a smart cookie and had closed countless deals by making many a man think she was a brainless twit. She would be out the door with the cash before anyone figured out she'd pulled the rug out from under them, and she always got the better deal.

"Stella, Randy is dead, and I nearly lost Candy because of that worthless drunk she had for a father. He screwed with her head, and I'll never forgive him for that. Deep down, I think she knows he lied about me and that he twisted the truth about the offer I made. She hated me for how long, all because her father wanted her to, and the kind of hurt that he put in her is so deep. I'm still having to chip away at the walls she's thrown up around her heart. I'm pretty sure they've always been there. I want her to know love, and sometimes it's better to leave all those ghosts and skeletons just where they are: dead and buried."

Neil glanced over at Candy as she slipped off Sables' halter and walked over to the shelter where Ambrose was hopping around excitedly. Ambrose had been stuck like glue to Sable since they were put together in this corral days ago.

"Well, her property is now yours. Does she know?"

Neil shook his head. "Not yet. I promised her I wouldn't touch it, and I had every intention of walking away from it." He breathed deeply, knowing Candy would be furious.

"But you found out that rich Texan was going to snatch it up and build condos up and down the beach."

"Yeah, couldn't have that. It'd kill her to see that piece of paradise desecrated."

Stella squeezed his arm. "So are we going to be seeing construction starting any time soon on that all-inclusive resort you have planned?"

He didn't miss the lightness that filled her voice. It was the same voice she used when she wanted in on some deal. "No," he said as he watched Candy heading straight for him with an easy smile and smoky eyes, with that magical spark that had been there for a week. It held their secret, their love. She looked so damn sexy in her pink skirt, which brushed her ankles, and her white tank top, with a thin belt at her waist. Her mile-long hair hung in waves, begging him to run his hands and fingers through it. "It'll be up to Candy what goes there. That's her baby, her place. She just doesn't know it yet."

"You're telling me you paid off her debt and you're giving her the property?" she asked. Neil stared down at the mischievous expression on Stella's face, and she patted his arm. "I expect a front-row seat at the wedding." Then she waved her hand and strode away, stopping to hug Candy.

"Hey, what was Stella doing here?" Candy asked as she went into the arms he held out to her.

"Oh, you know, catching up, seeing how we are."

She rested her chin on his chest and looked up at him. He couldn't help himself as he leaned down and kissed her lips.

"You know, before I scoop you up and take you up to bed, I want to ask you something." He had been waiting for the right time, and he watched the curiosity in her expression.

"What do you want to ask me?" She slid her hands over his butt and into his back pockets.

"Do you want a big or small wedding?"

Her eyes widened, and her face paled a bit before she said, "But you're supposed to ask me to marry you first."

Neil shoved his hand in his front pocket and went down on one knee. He held her hand in his and slid a pear-shaped diamond on her ring finger. "Candy McCrae, will you do me the honor of being my wife, the mother of my children, my lover, my best friend forever, until death do us part?"

Her expression crumbled, her lip trembled, and tears glossed over her eyes. She fought them back, blinking, and then cleared her throat and pressed a shaky hand to her lips as she shook her head and said, "Yes."

Neil lifted her in his arms and swung her around, then kissed her deeply. His cell phone rang in his shirt pocket. He rested his forehead against hers. "Bad timing." He yanked out the phone and looked at the call display. "Hey, Dad! Yeah, everything's fine." He squeezed Candy's waist and pulled her closer. "I got some great news." He gazed at the one woman he'd wanted for so long and said, "I'm getting married."

Turn the page for a sneak peek of
THE WEDDING the next book in THE OUTSIDER SERIES
Available in print, eBook and audio

A man who's always planned everything, and a woman who's struggled alone—The Wedding will change their lives forever.

In THE WEDDING, Candy McCrae has everything she could ever want, and she's about to marry the one man she's always loved. He has money, he's powerful, he's drop-dead gorgeous, and he has a very close, attentive family with babies, nieces, and nephews running everywhere. For the first time, Candy has someone making decisions for her. So why is she so nervous?

Candy is the one woman Neil has always wanted, a woman who doesn't care about flash and glitter and status, and he can't get her to the altar fast enough. He has plans for his bride-to-be. He wants a family, lots of children, and for her to be a part of his world, with all its money, power, and million-dollar deals. He'll look after her so she'll never have to struggle again, and he's planned and organized everything.

She goes along with it until the wedding, when she takes Neil's hand to be his wife, and what she's refused to share will change their lives forever.

—"I love the alpha males and their ever strong headed wives. They love hard and strong but forever. Don't miss out on how Neil and Candy finally get their happily ever after."

— REVIEWER, JANET

—*"Loved the deep family bond she gave all the characters even when the plots took them to fighting they stuck together. Something we don't find often today."*

— *REVIEWER, PEBBLES*

—*"Read the book-bittersweet but sometimes love has to go through fire to temper it and make it stronger."*

— *REVIEWER, AVTANNER*

—*"It has heartbreak like you wouldn't believe but most importantly, love that will have you reading it over and over. I got this one the day after I first read Neil and Candy's story. It really is a beautiful book."*

— *REVIEWER, RAMONA*

CHAPTER
ONE

"Wake up, sleepyhead." Neil slid his hand under the satiny sheet and over the inside of Candy McCrae's thigh. He was a rascal in the morning, and Candy was tired and could still feel the effects of being well loved the night before.

She rubbed her knuckles over her tired eyes and pressed into the corners, wiping the sleep away, then shoved her long, dark hair back. She hissed when he slid his hand higher and then pressed a kiss into her bare shoulder. "Neil, oh my God. I'm tired. What are you doing?" She gasped as his touch sent a jolt of pleasure through her.

He moved under the covers, touching her skin to skin, his hand skimming over her rounded cheeks and then across her flat stomach, up over her breasts. His touch was like a brand, saying to her without uttering one sound, "You're mine, my woman, and every part of you is mine alone to touch." She loved it! What woman wouldn't?

Candy tried to roll over to face Neil, but he stopped her with his body as he cupped her breast and pulled her against him. She slid her hand over the flexed muscles of his thighs, rubbing hair that was a mix of soft and mascu-line. He wouldn't let her turn to face him.

"Neil, I don't know if I can stand this. Let me touch you," she said, gasping when he nipped the back of her neck.

"Soon enough, but I mean to have you and taste every part of you," he murmured before running his tongue over her earlobe and nipping it with his teeth. Before she knew it, he'd rolled her over and draped her legs over his shoul-der, sliding into her. The light from the morning sun high-lighted gold flecks in the deep brown of his short hair, which was amazingly neat for a man who had spent most of the night inside Candy, doing all kinds of things to her that had her screaming out his name half a dozen times. It was a wonder she could still walk; the man was insatiable, and she stared into his brown eyes, which appeared to simmer the color of whiskey and burned into her as if he could read everything she tried to hide.

He held her head between his hands, pinning her down to have his way with her again. She couldn't move as he slid in and out, holding himself just above her, watching her, and she knew he could do anything to her and she'd let him. He loved it when she called out his name, and he'd wait until he knew she was nearly breaking apart before he'd tell her, "Say my name. Who do you belong to?"

She could never hold back. She couldn't stop herself as she screamed out, "Neil, oh my God, I'm yours!"

He filled what felt like every part of her, possessing her in a way that made her think she'd go mad, and in that same moment she knew that if he never touched her again, something inside her would slowly die.

After a moment, maybe two, they lay together; he was still inside her, his heartbeat matching the rhythm of hers and their breathing synchronized as one. She thought she heard voices outside, the sound of a car door slamming, but Neil didn't move. She ran her hands over his back, smoothing his tanned skin and taut, sculpted muscles with her fingertips. Still he didn't move, and she realized by his deep, relaxed breathing that he'd fallen asleep.

Candy glanced up at the window behind the bed and listened to the familiar voice of Maria, Neil's housekeeper, and two voices she'd never heard before. When Maria said, "How was your flight back, Señor Friessen, Señora?" Candy couldn't make out anything else, because she went into a full-blown panic. Neil's parents were here—now! A knot tightened in her stomach, a building anxiety, as she worried about what they would think of her. After all, she had nothing, and she wasn't sophisticated or worldly. Maybe they'd hate her, look down on her. She'd never said one word to Neil about her worries, because she knew he wouldn't have taken them seriously, but she couldn't help it. She stopped herself from waking Neil. Avoidance was sometimes a good thing. She decided she'd just hide out there and avoid them for as long as possible.

A loud, squeaky, braying and a crash as if something had shattered outside made Candy's blood turn to ice, and she shut her eyes. "Oh no, Ambrose," she muttered. Neil stirred, blinking just as a shout sounded below:

"What the hell is a donkey doing in my garden?"

The worst thing possible had just happened, and Candy widened her eyes in horror. She'd accomplished the one thing she had never wanted to do—start out on the wrong foot with Neil's mother.

ABOUT THE AUTHOR

"Lorhainne Eckhart is one of my go to authors when I want a guaranteed good book. So many twists and turns, but also so much love and such a strong sense of family."

— (LORA W., REVIEWER)

New York Times & USA Today bestseller Lorhainne Eckhart is best known for writing Raw Relatable Real Romance where "Morals and family are running themes." As one fan calls her, she is the "Queen of the family saga." (aherman) writing "the ups and downs of what goes on within a family but also with some suspense, angst and of course a bit of romance thrown in for good measure."

Follow Lorhainne on Bookbub to receive alerts on New Releases and Sales and join her mailing list at Lorhainne-Eckhart.com for her Monday Blog, all book news, giveaways and FREE reads. With over 120 books, audiobooks, and multiple series published and available at all, retailers now translated into six languages. She is a multiple recipient of the Readers' Favorite Award for Suspense and Romance, and lives in the Pacific Northwest on an island, is the mother of three, her oldest has autism and she is an advocate for never giving up on your dreams.

"Lorhainne Eckhart has this uncanny way of just hitting the spot every time with her books."

— (CAROLINE L., REVIEWER)

The O'Connells: *The O'Connells of Livingston, Montana are not your typical family. A riveting collection of stories surrounding the ups and downs of what goes on within a family but also with some suspense, angst and of course a bit of romance thrown in for good measure. "I thought I loved the Friessens, but I absolutely adore the O'Connell's. Each and every book has different genres of stories, but the one thing in common is how she is able to wrap it around the family, which is the heart of each story." (C. Logue)*

The Friessens: *An emotional big family romance series, the Friessen family siblings find their relationships tested, lay their hearts on the line, and discover lasting love! "Lorhainne Eckhart is one of my go to authors when I want* a guaranteed good book. So many twists and turns, but also so much love and such a strong sense of family." (Lora W., Reviewer)

The Parker Sisters: The Parker Sisters are a close-knit family, and like any other family they have their ups and downs. Eckhart has crafted another intense family drama... "The character development is outstanding, and the emotional investment is high..." (Aherman, Reviewer)

The McCabe Brothers: Join the five McCabe siblings on their journeys to the dark and dangerous side of love! An intense, exhilarating collection of romantic thrillers you won't want to miss. — "Eckhart has a new series that is definitely worth the read. The queen of the family saga started this series with a spin-off of her wildly successful Friessen series." From a Readers' Favorite award—winning author and "queen of the family saga" (Aherman)

Billy Jo McCabe Mystery: The social worker and the cop, an unlikely couple drawn together on a small, secluded Pacific Northwest island where nothing is as it seems. Protecting the innocent comes at a cost, and what seems to be a sleepy, quiet town is anything but.

The Wilde Brothers: Meet the Wilde brothers of Idaho. Joe, Logan, Ben, Jake & Samuel in this big family romance series.

Lorhainne loves to hear from her readers! You can connect with me at:
www.LorhainneEckhart.com
lorhainneeckhart.le@gmail.com

ALSO BY LORHAINNE ECKHART

The Outsider Series
The Forgotten Child (Brad and Emily)
A Baby and a Wedding *(An Outsider Series Short)*
Fallen Hero (Andy, Jed, and Diana)
The Search *(An Outsider Series Short)*
The Awakening (Andy and Laura)
Secrets (Jed and Diana)
Runaway (Andy and Laura)
Overdue *(An Outsider Series Short)*
The Unexpected Storm (Neil and Candy)
The Wedding (Neil and Candy)

The Friessens: A New Beginning
The Deadline (Andy and Laura)
The Price to Love (Neil and Candy)
A Different Kind of Love (Brad and Emily)
A Vow of Love, A Friessen Family Christmas

The Friessens
The Reunion
The Bloodline (Andy & Laura)
The Promise (Diana & Jed)
The Business Plan (Neil & Candy)
The Decision (Brad & Emily)
First Love (Katy)
Family First
Leave the Light On
In the Moment
In the Family

In the Silence
In the Charm
Unexpected Consequences
It Was Always You
The First Time I Saw You
Welcome to My Arms
Welcome to Boston
I'll Always Love You
Ground Rules
A Reason to Breathe
You Are My Everything
Anything For You
The Homecoming
Stay Away From My Daughter
The Bad Boy
A Place of Our Own
The Visitor
All About Devon
Long Past Dawn
How to Heal a Heart
Keep Me In Your Heart

The O'Connells

The Neighbor
The Third Call
The Secret Husband
The Quiet Day
The Commitment
The Missing Father
The Hometown Hero
Justice
The Family Secret
The Fallen O'Connell
The Return of the O'Connells

And The She Was Gone
The Stalker
The O'Connell Family Christmas
The Girl Next Door
Broken Promises
The Gatekeeper
The Hunted

The McCabe Brothers

Don't Stop Me (Vic)
Don't Catch Me (Chase)
Don't Run From Me (Aaron)
Don't Hide From Me (Luc)
Don't Leave Me (Claudia)
Out of Time

A Billy Jo McCabe Mystery

Nothing As it Seems
Hiding in Plain Sight
The Cold Case
The Trap
Above the Law
The Stranger at the Door
The Children
The Last Stand
The Charity
The Sacrifice

The Street Fighter

Finding Home

The Wilde Brothers

The One (Joe and Margaret)
The Honeymoon, A Wilde Brothers Short

Friendly Fire (Logan and Julia)
Not Quite Married, A Wilde Brothers Short
A Matter of Trust (Ben and Carrie)
The Reckoning, A Wilde Brothers Christmas
Traded (Jake)
Unforgiven (Samuel)
The Holiday Bride

Married in Montana

His Promise
Love's Promise
A Promise of Forever

The Parker Sisters

Thrill of the Chase
The Dating Game
Play Hard to Get
What We Can't Have
Go Your Own Way
A June Wedding

Kate & Walker

One Night
Edge of Night
Last Night

Walk the Right Road Series

The Choice
Lost and Found
Merkaba
Bounty
Blown Away: The Final Chapter
He Came Back

CPSIA information can be obtained
at www.ICGtesting.com
Printed in the USA
BVHW041206250822
645505BV00003B/219